THE HIGH COUNTRY

VICTORIA *Wyngate*

Published by Victoria Wyngate
Copyright © 2018 Victoria Wyngate
All Rights Reserved

Copyright

Published by Victoria Wyngate
Copyright © 2018 Victoria Wyngate
First Edition: 2018
Cover by Just Write Creations
Editing and Proofreading by Emma Mack at Ultra Editing Co.
No part of this publication may be reproduced, stored in or introduced into retrieval systems, or transmitted in any form, or by any means (electronic, mechanical, photocopying, recording or otherwise) without the prior written permission from the author of this book.
This is a work of fiction. Names, character, places, brands, media and incidents are either the product of the author's imagination or are completely fictional.
Any trademarks referenced herein are used without the trademark holder(s) permission. The use of these trademarks is not authorized, associated with, or sponsored by the trademark holder(s).

All Rights Reserved

DEDICATION

To my Husband, I love you with all that I am and all that I will ever be. Thank you for supporting me in this endeavor. To both of my daughters, I love you more than you will ever know. To my grandson, you will always be Grandma's shining star.

Emma, thank you for believing in me at a time when I had trouble believing in myself.

To all my friends, both old and new, you guys mean the world to me. I couldn't have made it this far without all your love and support.

Victoria

DISCLAIMER

Any similarity to any person or persons referenced in this work is strictly from the author's imagination. Any similarities to any person, either living or dead, are unintentional and purely co-incidental. Any locations referenced herein are, again, the product of the authors imagination and are not intended to depict any actual geographical or physical location. The trademarks referenced in the work are used for reference only and are used without the trademark holder's permission.

AUTHORS NOTE

This novel contains sexual content and scenes depicting peril. It may not be suitable for readers under the age of 18. Reader discretion is therefore advised.

PROLOGUE

TREVOR BRIGSTON WAS speeding down Fairmount Avenue and the speedometer registered at over 90 miles per hour. He'd driven this recklessly only one other time in his lifetime and right now he was in the same kind of hurry. He was probably going to be stopped by the police. Probably wind up with a ticket, but right now that was the least of his worries.

From the passenger seat of his truck came a loud moan, followed by a muffled short squeal. The next thing he heard from the woman sitting to his right, his wife Elizabeth, was a loud piercing scream of, "TREVOR!"

"We're almost there, sweetheart. Just breathe," he coached.

"BUT IT HURTS!" she screamed. Her breathing was coming in the form of sharp, ragged, gasps and squeals as he pulled into the emergency lane of the Cheyenne Memorial Hospital. He stopped the truck under the awning of the emergency entrance, ran through the front sliding glass doors and returned with a wheelchair.

Running to the truck, he opened the passenger door and helped her out of the truck and to a semi-standing position.

She had only taken two steps and was turning to sit in the wheelchair when her body was racked by another spasm. She froze in place and doubled over, grabbing her distended abdomen.

"They're coming faster," she whispered through the pain. Trevor supported her until the spasm subsided and gently slid her into the chair and wheeled her across the threshold of the double glass doors and over to the check-in desk.

"Please, help her!" he said to the first person he saw. A male nurse in blue surgical scrubs. The nurse looked over at Elizabeth, who was clearly in pain.

"How far apart are they?" he queried.

"Right before we walked out the front door to come here they were at four minutes apart and her water broke on the way to the truck. They're coming a lot closer now, but I couldn't time them. I forgot my watch," Trevor replied.

"Bring her right in here," he said to Trevor. "We'll get her information after we get her situated into a room. I'm Andy. I'm the charge nurse on duty tonight. We'll take good care of her. Melanie, can you get…" he paused.

"Trevor…Trevor Brigston," Trevor continued for him.

"Get Mr. Brigston a set of scrubs and show him to the nearest place where he can change?" Andy continued.

"Sure thing," said Melanie. "Right this way."

Melanie escorted Trevor down a small hallway to a small alcove. It was the family restroom. She handed him a set of disposable scrubs and pointed to the door.

"You'll need to don these as quickly as possible, as it seems that your child is in a hurry to enter this world, like, NOW! Once you've finished that, we'll let you see your wife," she said.

"Her name is Elizabeth, but she likes to be called Beth," he said as he took the scrubs. Changing as quickly as he could, he stepped back into the hallway and followed Melanie to find Beth.

THE HIGH COUNTRY

He walked into the delivery room as several nurses were hooking Beth up to all sorts of monitoring equipment.

The thought of the pain his wife was currently enduring terrified him. He watched as the anesthesiologist started administering her epidural.

The expression of pain on Beth's face changed to one of peace as the epidural took effect and the pain gradually subsided. She looked over to Trevor and extended her hand to him.

He took it as he whispered into her ear, "I love you."

"I love you too," she replied. She couldn't feel the pain of the contractions, but she still felt the urge to push. This child was definitely in a hurry to meet his parents.

Beth's obstetrician, Marion Shapiro, came into the delivery room and checked on the progress of Beth's labor and contractions.

"Okay Beth, it's showtime. I am going to need you to give me a big push with the next contraction," she instructed.

Beth felt her stomach muscles contract, but there was no pain. She dipped her chin to her chest, as she had been instructed, and pushed as hard as she could.

"That's it. You are doing great," said Dr. Shapiro.

"Alright, give me one more big push."

Beth assumed the position again and gritted her teeth as she pushed hard. Trevor was standing at Beth's head and a nurse handed him a cold cloth. Trevor looked at her with a puzzled expression.

"Mop her brow, talk to her and help keep her calm," the nurse said as if answering an unasked question.

He took the cloth and gently dabbed Beth's forehead with it as another contraction racked her small frame.

"Beth, I need you to give me your biggest and best effort. Now PUSH!" Dr. Shapiro instructed.

With one final push from Beth, the world welcomed Elijah Trevor Brigston at 11:35 p.m. on August 15th, 2016. Seven pounds, eleven ounces and twenty-one inches long.

They had decided to call him 'Eli' for short.

After recovering in the hospital for two days, the trio went home to introduce Eli to his big sister, Caroline, and the rest of the people awaiting him at The High Country Acres.

CHAPTER ONE

LIFE AT THE ranch was chaos shortly after the new parents introduced the latest addition to the rest of the household. Eli was up frequently during the night. He was demanding to either be fed or changed. He slept most of the day, even with the constant jostling of changing and handing him off for others to hold.

Everyone in the household was exhausted by the end of the first week, especially Beth.

She seemed to become fatigued a lot more easily now, but she just attributed it to the strain of the delivery and the post-partum recovery. She tried to rest as much as she could, or at least as much as caring for Eli would allow.

She was nursing him every three hours. Trevor would bring her trays of food and put them on the bedside table. Beth would look at the tray, but barely touched anything on it. She forced herself to eat because she knew that she needed to, for Eli's sake.

Beth's weight dropped significantly within the first few weeks after Eli's birth. Her skin became so pale and gaunt that Trevor became concerned about her health.

He consulted Beth's doctor, who just attributed the weight loss to the normal post-partum changes. She assured the family that everything was progressing normally. Beth was fine, and they had nothing to worry about.

As Beth was putting Eli into his crib one morning and she suddenly became so dizzy that she almost fell while still cradling the baby. Trevor just happened to be stepping into the room at the time and caught Beth by the shoulders and held her.

"Easy there, Honey. Let me help you," he said as he took Eli from her arms and placed him gently into his crib.

Beth clung to the side railing of the crib in an effort to steady herself.

"Are you okay?" he asked. "You look awfully pale."

"I just got real dizzy all of a sudden."

"I'm not surprised," he said. "You've hardly eaten anything since you came home from the hospital."

"I know. I don't understand why I don't seem to have an appetite anymore."

"I think we need to make another trip to the doctor," Trevor said as he helped her to a rocking chair in the corner of the nursery.

"*No. Please, not again,*" Beth pleaded. "They didn't find anything the last time. What makes you think this time will be any different?" she asked.

He knelt in front of her. "Something is wrong with you and I won't rest until they find out what it is," he said adamantly.

"I'm making you another appointment first thing in the morning. But right now, I think you should rest. I'll take care of Eli, when he wakes," he said as he took her arm and helped her up and down the hall to their room.

"I'm sure it's nothing to worry about," she said as she lay down on their bed. "But I have to admit, I am tired. Maybe I *will* take a little nap."

THE HIGH COUNTRY

Beth's nap lasted for fourteen hours. Trevor had checked on her periodically. As long as she was sleeping peacefully, he let her rest.

She obviously needs it right now, he thought. Eli roused several times and was fed, changed and rocked back to sleep by his father.

Trevor was sitting in an armchair in the far corner of their room when he heard Beth start to stir. He jumped up and ran over to the bed.

"Hey, there's my sleeping beauty," he said as he sat gently on the side of the bed.

"*Eli*," she said as she tried to rise.

"He's fine and sleeping peacefully."

"What time is it?" she asked sleepily.

"7:00 a.m."

"WHAT!" she exclaimed, shocked by his answer.

"I was just going down for a short nap. I must have been more exhausted than I thought," she continued.

"As soon as the doctor's office opens, I'm calling to make you an appointment. I'm really worried about you sweetheart."

"I'm probably just a little anemic," Beth countered. "You worry too much."

At 1:30 p.m. that same afternoon, Trevor and Beth pulled into the office of Dr. Jonathan Lawrence, Internal Medicine.

After explaining her symptoms, Beth was subjected to a battery of blood tests. Dr. Lawrence came back into the room soon as the lab tech was leaving. He walked over and sat on the rollout stool to talk to Beth.

"As soon as my nurse gets here we'll start the physical examination," Dr. Lawrence said.

"We'll need to make you an appointment to go to the hospital for a CT scan. Your weight loss and lack of appetite combined with the dizziness and fatigue are causes for concern. I'll write an order for the scan and you'll need to see Tina up front to schedule it as soon as possible."

"Thanks Doc," Trevor said as they followed the doctor toward the front desk.

"That's Tina over there," the doctor said as he pointed to a tall blonde sitting at the corner desk.

"Make sure you schedule a follow-up with me in two weeks to discuss the results. If you have any immediate problems before then, feel free to make another appointment sooner than that. Otherwise, I'll see you in two weeks." Dr. Lawrence said before he walked into another exam room.

They walked over to Tina's desk and took a seat. They looked up as a short brunette woman walked up and handed Tina a slip of paper.

"Thanks, Elaine," Tina said.

"Don't mention it," Elaine said as she walked away.

Trevor pulled back into the driveway of High Country Acres a little over three hours later. Tina had scheduled the CT scan for 9:00 a.m. on Thursday. That was the earliest time that the hospital had available and they took it.

Emily, their live-in housekeeper and cook, met the couple at the door with a screaming Eli in her arms.

"This little man has been crying for over twenty minutes solid. Nothing I do will quiet him," she said.

"He's hungry. I'll take him," Beth said, holding out her arms. Emily handed the baby to Beth and he immediately began nuzzling at her chest.

"See," Beth said.

THE HIGH COUNTRY

She took him into a small room off the foyer so that she could nurse him.

"What did the doctor say?" Emily asked Trevor as Beth left the room.

"Not much of anything," he said angrily. "We have to wait on the results of the blood tests. She's also scheduled for a CT Scan on Thursday. Then we still have to wait another two weeks for the follow-up with the doctor. Hopefully, we'll know more then."

"Let's hope for everybody's sake we get some good news then," Emily replied. "Oh, supper will be ready in twenty minutes."

At 8:30 a.m. Thursday morning, Trevor and Beth pulled into the parking lot of the Cheyenne Memorial Hospital Imaging Center, thirty minutes ahead of Beth's scheduled appointment. They walked in through the double sliding glass doors and signed in at the reception desk.

Almost an hour later, they finally called Beth's name. The radiology technician instructed Trevor to wait where he was.

He picked up a magazine from the table in front of him. It was a Woman's Day that was over three years old. He sighed and threw it back onto the table. He stood and started pacing the floor.

Half an hour and a path worn in the floor later Beth emerged through the door at the back of the room.

"How'd it go?" he asked expectantly.

"As well as could be expected, but they didn't tell me anything. We still have to wait until the follow up appointment. I just hope the waiting *is* the hardest part of this whole ordeal like that old song says," she answered sarcastically.

Trevor grabbed her in a strong embrace. *"We'll get through, whatever this is, together,"* he promised.

He held her tightly as they went back to the truck. He reached for her hand and held it tightly during the drive back to the ranch.

Neither of them spoke, *not one word.*

CHAPTER TWO

THE NEXT TWO weeks passed at a snail's pace, but the appointment date for the follow-up finally arrived. Their drive into town seemed to take forever, but in actuality, it was only half an hour. Signing in at the front desk, they held hands as they took their seats.

Twenty minutes later, the medical assistant called her name. They were escorted to an exam room, asked a few more questions and were left to wait again.

Doctor Lawrence entered the room with her chart in his hands. He pulled out the rolling stool from under the desk, sat down on it and slid himself over to face the couple. Their hands were gripped tightly.

"I don't mean to alarm you, but I don't usually sugar coat things either. So, I will get right to the point. There are several findings in your lab work and CT scan that are of great concern to me," he blurted.

The look of concern was clear on both of their faces. "I'm not sure I like where this is going…" Trevor started.

"Hush, Honey. Please just let him finish," Beth interrupted.

"Thank you," the doctor continued. "Your HCG level is elevated and that usually occurs during pregnancy. Your pelvic exam from two weeks ago showed no evidence of one. That combined with the fact that you stated that your last menstrual cycle was a week before we last met," he said. "I think we can rule that out."

Both Trevor and Beth just looked at him and nodded. The doctor continued, "That being the case there has to be another solution. Those results combined with the CT scan findings, I'm going to refer Beth back to her OB/GYN."

Both Trevor and Beth looked up at the doctor, hanging on his every word.

Doctor Lawrence continued, "The CT scan revealed a 3 cm solid mass on your left ovary. It may be nothing, but I would feel better if we could get you in for a biopsy as soon as possible."

The couple nodded, but they didn't speak. Instead they waited for the doctor to continue.

"I think it would be best if Tina scheduled the appointment. Our office can probably get you seen sooner," he said. "Just stop by her desk on the way out please."

CHAPTER THREE

TREVOR WALKED INTO their foyer and was greeted by a loud and excited squeal of, "DADDY!" He turned to see their daughter Caroline running into the room with her small arms stretched open wide. Bending down he scooped her up and hugged her tightly.

"Daddy, you're squishing me," she complained. "Oh, I'm sorry pumpkin. I just missed you so much and Daddy really needs your hugs right now."

"Is Mommy okay?" she asked.

Beth spoke first, "Mommy is just fine sweetheart. Have you had your lunch?"

"Yep," she answered, "Emily made my favorite."

"Oh, no! Not peanut butter and jelly *again*?" Beth said with a strained lilt in her voice.

"Yep," Caroline said again nodding.

"If I'm not mistaken, it looks like strawberry this time," said Beth as she pointed to a dribble of jam on the front of Caroline's pretty pink dress.

Caroline nodded happily as she reached for her mother. "Mommy, looks like you need my hugs too," she said.

"Boy do I ever, Minion," Beth replied.

Caroline giggled at the reference to the characters from her favorite movie. Beth always called her 'Minion' during their tender moments together.

Trevor passed the five-year-old to her mother. Beth held Caroline against her chest tightly kissing the top of her head, inhaling the aromas of baby shampoo and fresh strawberry jam. She loved those scents. A tear rolled down her cheek as she squeezed her daughter tight.

"Mommy, now *you're* squishing me," Caroline whined.

"I'm sorry baby. I just love you so much," Beth said as she eased her hold on Caroline.

"I love you too, Mommy. Can I go play now?" Caroline asked innocently.

"Sure, Minion, just don't get anything *else* on that pretty dress, okay?" said Beth as she put her down.

"Okay," said Caroline as she ran toward the back of the house.

Beth knew full well where Caroline was headed. She was going to the corral. They had just added a brown Quarter Horse mare to their team and Caroline had taken an instant liking to her the first time she laid eyes on her. Trevor had even let Caroline name the mare.

Caroline had taken one look at the mare and said just one word, "Chocolate". And 'Chocolate' the mare had remained.

Beth's biopsy was scheduled for the following Tuesday at 9:00 am. She was visibly shaking as Trevor pulled into the parking deck of the surgery center. He shut off the engine but didn't move from his seat. Placing his right hand on her cheek, he looked her in the eye and said with conviction, "We will get through whatever this is together. I promise."

"I know," she said, "But I'm still scared."

THE HIGH COUNTRY

"I will be there the moment you wake up. My ugly mug will be the first thing you see."

"I love you," she whispered as she covered his hand with hers.

"I love you too, but we've gotta go or, we're gonna be late."

They checked in at the reception desk and waited. Beth's name was called, and she was taken into a pre-op suite where her intravenous lines were started. Trevor was by her side the entire time and she was given a sedative to help calm her.

Her stomach growled as they waited for her to be taken back. She shrugged her shoulders and said, "Sorry, but I'm hungry."

"I promise that you can have the biggest steak you can imagine, when we get home."

"I'm gonna hold you to that mister!" she admonished.

"I made you a promise, didn't I?" was all he said as the nurses came and wheeled her away to the operating room.

It was over an hour before the doctor came out to the waiting room to speak to Trevor. He took a seat beside him and paused for a moment before he said, "I'm afraid I don't have good news for you."

"What are we looking at Doc?"

"The biopsy of the mass on Beth's ovary came back malignant. I had the lab rush the tests and I'm afraid that it's stage two ovarian cancer, almost to stage three. Before we go any further, I recommend bringing Beth out of the anesthesia. You both need to make an informed decision as to our course of treatment. What I'm recommending is a complete and radical hysterectomy, followed by aggressive chemotherapy, but I feel that she needs to be involved in this decision."

Trevor didn't say anything. He simply put his face into the palm of his hands. The doctor had lost him at the word 'malignant'. All Trevor thought about was Beth. He couldn't lose her.

Beth opened her eyes groggily and licked her lips. Her throat was dry, and she desperately wanted a drink of water.

She looked over to Trevor and asked, "Can I have some water, please?"

"I'll wet your lips with a towel, but I'm afraid I can't let you drink anything right now," he answered.

"Why?" she asked weakly.

"We have to make a decision, right now, Honey. They told me that the mass they found on your ovary is malignant. They needed a decision on the course of your treatment. It was a decision that I was not willing to make, at least not on my own. Not without talking to you first.

You have to listen closely sweetheart. Are you listening to me?" he asked.

She nodded that she was.

"Honey, they need to perform a complete hysterectomy on you because they said that it's stage two ovarian cancer," he said reluctantly.

The look of fear in her eyes was unmistakable.

"I wasn't willing to make that call on my own. That decision should be yours," he said.

"If that's what needs to be done and it's my consent you need, I give it. Do whatever it takes."

Trevor noticed that the doctor had been standing quietly waiting by the door. Almost eager for her decision.

"You heard her," Trevor said as he signed the consent, "Do it."

THE HIGH COUNTRY

Following her surgery, Beth recovered slowly. The chemotherapy that she'd had to endure had weakened her to the point that she was bed-ridden most of the time.

The nausea was unending. She longed to hold her children but was cautioned that even the simplest virus could wreak havoc with her immune system. She couldn't risk it. Not quite yet.

Trevor rigged up a closed-circuit television system, where she could talk to the children without exposing her to bacteria or viruses that could cause her further health problems.

To Beth, that was almost unbearable. She wanted to hold her children. To be able to read them bed-time stories and tuck them in at night, but all of that would have to wait.

For months, Beth endured the trips to the Oncology Center twice a week for her chemotherapy appointments. The treatments that were supposed to be saving her life were instead making her weaker. Her hair was falling out by the hand-full each time she showered. The constant nausea and fatigue she experienced were taking their toll on her. All she ever felt like doing now was sleeping.

Trevor had bought her some decorative scarves which she wrapped loosely around her head to cover her thinning locks.

Caroline liked the colorful scarves so much that she insisted her father buy her matching ones. She wore them tied tightly around her golden curls.

"Look Mommy, we match today," said Caroline as she pointed to her head.

"I see that Minion," Beth replied weakly.

"Mommy, are you getting better?" Caroline asked innocently.

"Well, I sure hope so. They're giving me lots of medicine to help with that," Beth replied.

Unfortunately, her subsequent tests revealed that the cancer had metastasized to her liver, bladder and intestines.

All of the medicines and chemotherapy that she had endured had done little to stop the cancer that was wreaking havoc in Beth's body.

Beth's oncologist informed them that they wanted to try a new but experimental treatment. The doctor told the couple that there had been a 25% success rate with this new treatment.

The treatment would mean traveling to Europe and there was no guarantee of her going into remission.

Trevor and Beth decided that it would be best to stop the treatments and allow her to spend what little quality time that she had left with her husband and children.

The next few months were extremely difficult for Trevor as he could do nothing except watch as Beth continued to grow weaker as the disease ravaged her body.

During one of her good days, Beth called Trevor to her bedside.

She looked up weakly as he entered the room, walked over to the bedside and sat down on the on the side of the king size bed.

"I'm here, Honey," he said, trying to manage a smile. Inside he was screaming, crying and otherwise in utter turmoil, but he couldn't let her see that.

Beth reached out her hand, took his and brought it to her lips. She kissed it but didn't release her grip.

"I want you to promise me something," she said softly, patting his hand. She raised her face to look at him.

"Anything, just ask for it."

THE HIGH COUNTRY

"Promise me that you will find love again. I know that you will grieve, but I don't want it to consume you. I want you to find someone that will love you and our children as much as I do."

"I can't promise you that," he admitted.

"You said *'anything',*" she reminded him. "Promise me?"

"It might take me a while, but I promise that I'll try. That is the best I can do right now. To promise to try."

Beth nodded her head in acceptance of his promise and closed her eyes.

Trevor bent and kissed her gently on the forehead.

"I love you," he said. "What am I going to do without you?" Beth opened her eyes and looked at him.

"You will be the awesome father that I know you are and you will help our children to remember me. *That's what you'll do."*

"You just rest now," Trevor said tenderly as he kissed her forehead again. He felt the tears welling in his eyes and he didn't want to upset her. He stood and walked toward the door.

"I'll be back to check on you a little later, just sleep now."

A week later Beth lost her battle with the dreadful disease on May 26th, 2017. She passed away quietly at 4:52 p.m. surrounded by her loving family and friends who huddled together and wept.

She was only thirty-two.

Caroline had just turned six. Eli was only nine months old.

CHAPTER FOUR

IN THE WEEKS following Beth's funeral service, Trevor tried to shield his children from the extent of his grief by completely immersing himself in the day-to-day operation of the ranch.

Today was no exception.

He woke with the first morning light and tip-toed to the nursery sticking his head inside. Eli was sleeping peacefully. He had awoken only once during the night and Emily had tended to him.

I'm going to have to give that poor woman a raise, he thought, *she surely deserves a big one.*

He didn't check in on Caroline. She's such a light sleeper that she would've been wide awake with the first squeak of the hinges on the door. She had a busy day scheduled at school and she needed the few extra minutes of sleep this morning.

Despite getting up with Eli earlier this morning, he found Emily in the kitchen bustling about between the counter and two skillets steaming on the stove.

She turned to face him as she heard him enter the room.

THE HIGH COUNTRY

"Breakfast won't be ready for another ten minutes," she said.

"No time for a sit-down breakfast," Trevor said. "I'm planning on riding up to the northern fence line to check the damage from the storm that passed through. Gotta make sure the cows don't wander off," he continued, pouring himself a cup of the freshly brewed coffee.

"But you can't do that on an empty stomach," Emily scolded. "Are you taking the four-wheeler?"

Trevor picked up a piece of toast from a plate on the counter and took a large bite and began chewing noisily.

"There, breakfast," he chided as he put the toast to his lips and took another bite.

"Dry toast?" she asked as she raised her eyebrow.

"And coffee," he replied holding up his cup. "And to answer your question, no. I'm taking Chocolate."

"*Candy?*" Emily asked.

"No, Caroline's horse," he chuckled. "She needs the exercise and the terrain is too steep and rough for the four-wheeler."

"Oh, that's right," said Emily as she put her hand on her chin. "I forgot she'd named her horse that." She turned back to one of the skillets and stirred the eggs she was scrambling.

"Are you alright?" Trevor asked as he sat his cup on the counter and walked over to her. He put his hand on her shoulder, a looked of concern creasing his brow.

"Don't you fret about me. I'm just fine," she admonished. She turned and wiped her hands on the dish towel. "I need to go and check on the children. Caroline is gonna miss the bus if she doesn't get up and get ready soon," she continued.

"I've gotta go myself. I need to get a look at the damage and make a list of the supplies we're gonna need," he replied.

He popped the last bite of the toast into his mouth, drank the last of the coffee and put the mug into the sink.

He turned and walked out the back door. Emily turned off the burners of the stove and went upstairs to rouse Caroline. She just hoped the little girl was in a better mood than she had been at bath time last night.

Trevor saddled Chocolate at dawn and was riding the upper fence line as the sun reached the top of the trees. He noticed several points along the outer perimeter of the fencing that had been broken by some downed trees.

Some sections of the fencing had rusted or were missing nails and the wood had become rotten.

"Shit!" he said aloud. *The repairs will take the better part of a week*, he thought. Not to mention getting the materials up here. He pulled the reins to stop the horse and dismounted. Walking over to a small oak sapling he secured the horse to it.

In frustration he ran his hand through his dark brown wavy locks and slapped the hand on the denim of his jeans. He had been planning on rotating the cattle to this side of the pasture for better grazing. The move would have to wait until the repairs could be completed.

Emily tip-toed up the stairs and slowly opened the door to Caroline's room. Quietly walking over to the side of the bed she touched the child on the shoulder.

"Caroline, Honey. You need to get up and get dressed or you're gonna miss your bus," she said as she stroked Caroline's shoulder.

"I'm not going," Caroline answered with her head still beneath the covers.

"And why not?" Emily still had her hand on the girl's arm.

Caroline turned over and whisked the covers from her head with one swift motion. This action startled Emily and she flinched.

"Everybody there is mean to me," the small child confided.

"Mean? How?" Emily asked.

"They make fun of me and call me names."

"Have you talked to your teacher about it?" "Yeah, but I don't think she believed me," Caroline answered sheepishly.

"Why would you say that?" Emily asked.

"She just said they didn't mean it, but I know they did," the small child replied.

Their conversation was interrupted by a loud wail from the nursery. Emily looked toward the hallway then back to Caroline.

"I'll be back in five minutes and you need to be ready for school young lady," Emily scolded as she rose from the bed and left the room. She said over her shoulder at the doorway, "Make that four minutes."

Caroline reluctantly went to her closet and began picking out her clothes, throwing what she didn't want to wear on the floor at her feet. After selecting a frilly pink dress and matching tights, she began to get ready, but she wasn't very happy about it.

Five minutes later Emily returned to Caroline's room with a freshly changed Eli. As she crossed the threshold to the room she heard the unmistakable sound of airbrakes hissing outside.

Walking over to the window she pulled back the curtain and looked outside. She was just in time to see the bright yellow bus pulling away from the end of the driveway.

"Well missy, just what I was afraid of. Looks like we've missed your bus," said Emily as she turned to face the little girl.

"Good. Then I don't have to go," the girl replied as she started to pull her dress back over her head.

"Not so fast," Emily retorted. "All that means is that I have to drive you. Let's go."

"You're no fun," said Caroline as she grabbed her backpack.

"School first, fun later," Emily promised.

As they reached the kitchen Caroline suddenly blurted, "Wait!"

"For what?" asked Emily.

"I want to get a carrot for Chocolate," Caroline replied as she opened the door to the refrigerator.

"That's gonna have to wait young lady," said Emily.

"Why won't you let me give her a carrot? It'll only take a minute," Caroline queried sullenly.

"It's not that I won't. I can't. She's not here."

"Where is she?"

"Your father rode her up to the upper pasture early this morning before the sun came up. She'll just have to wait for her treat. Now let's go before you're really late for school," Emily said as she opened the door and they stepped outside.

Emily couldn't help but notice the dark storm clouds on the horizon.

Not again, she thought, *not on the heels of that last one.*

Trevor looked up as the first rumble of thunder cascaded across the horizon. A bolt of lightning illuminated the dark clouds that layered across the sky.

Not again, he thought, *not now.*

"Guess we'd better head back girl," he said as he walked over and rubbed the neck of the grazing horse. He untied her reins and put the toe of his boot into the stirrup and hoisted his other leg over the saddle and onto the back of the horse. Clicking his tongue as he pulled on the reins, he turned the horse toward the ranch house.

THE HIGH COUNTRY

Just hope I can get us back before it hits, he thought.

He gently nudged the horse's side with his heel to get her into a run. The rain started coming down hard as they neared the barn. By the time they were inside it they were both soaked.

"I'm sorry girl," Trevor said to the horse as he dismounted. He loosened the harness of the saddle and removed it and the saddle blanket in one movement.

The blanket was soaked through, so he laid it out over the rail of one of the nearby stalls to dry. He left the harness on the horse and tied the loose ends of the reins to a metal ring hanging on the outside of her stall.

There was a storage cabinet at the far end of the barn for towels, blankets, combs and brushes. He walked over to the cabinet and removed two towels, a brush and another blanket and went back to the horse.

He started toweling off the horse, soothing her as he did.

"I know you have to be cold girl. I know I am, but I think this should warm you up a bit," he said as he rubbed the towel over her flank. When both towels were saturated he started brushing the horse, still talking to her.

"Our little girl will be sore with me if I let you get sick," he said. He finished brushing Chocolate, and threw the blanket over her back. This blanket had fasteners that kept it in place.

After fastening the blanket, he untied the horse and led her into her stall. Latching the door, he went over to the nail on the side of her stall that held her feed bucket. He scooped a small amount of oats into her bucket.

"That'll have to do you for now," he said as he stroked Chocolate's neck as she ate. "I have to get cleaned up myself."

He turned and walked through the rain up to the ranch house.

Emily pulled the car into the parking lot of the Caroline's school and shut off the engine.

"Unbuckle yourself while I get Eli out of his car seat," she told Caroline.

Caroline sat in her booster seat, unmoving.

"Come on young lady. That storm is going to hit any minute. We don't have time for this," Emily scolded.

Caroline reluctantly unfastened her seatbelt and got out of the car. A loud clap of thunder rumbled the sky as the first drops of rain landed on Caroline's face.

"See, now hurry up or we're gonna get soaked," said Emily. As they hurried across the parking lot the sky opened up and let loose. The rain drops were big and were coming down fast.

They entered the building as the tardy bell rang. The hallway was empty as they made their way to the main office.

"I'll have to sign you in again," Emily said as she opened the door and they walked inside the main office. The receptionist looked up as they approached the desk.

"Can I help you?" she asked.

"Yes ma'am," replied Emily. "This is Caroline Brigston. I'm afraid she missed the bus this morning and I had a hard time getting her ready today. I'm here to sign her in." Caroline gave Emily a cross look but said nothing.

"Are you her mother?" the woman asked.

"No, ma'am," Emily responded. "Her mother passed away a few months back."

"Oh, I'm sorry to hear that," the woman said apologetically. "Just sign this and I'll get her a slip to take to her teacher."

CHAPTER FIVE

CAROLINE SULKED DOWN the hall, not looking forward to the questions she knew she was going to get from her teacher, Molly Swanson.

She reached the classroom and hesitantly gripped the door knob.

Taking a deep breath, she turned the knob and walked into the room. Just as she crossed the threshold a loud clap of thunder rattled across the sky. Caroline couldn't help it, she jumped at the sound.

"There you are," said Ms. Swanson. "I was ready to mark you absent. Don't you have a few papers for me?" Molly held out her hand, palm up, toward the small child.

"Yes ma'am," Caroline replied sheepishly as she approached the desk. She held out the tardy slip that she had been given at the office.

"What about the other slips I sent home with you?" asked Ms. Swanson as she took the offered slip of paper.

"I forgot them," Caroline answered.

"Forgot, huh? Okay, I guess I can let you turn them in tomorrow, but just make sure that you do. Now, please go ahead and take your seat," replied Ms. Swanson as she pointed to the empty desk.

Molly made a mental note to call Caroline's parents and ask about the slips and to inform them of her recent behavioral issues.

Emily came into the kitchen from the mud room as Trevor turned the corner of the dining room wall on the other side of the room.

She was holding Eli in her left arm and shaking the rain off her umbrella with her right.

"What are both of you doing out in weather like this?" Trevor asked.

"Caroline missed her bus again. I had to drive her this morning," Emily answered as she handed Eli to Trevor. Eli Stretched out his tiny arms toward his father as Trevor took him from.

Emily removed her raincoat and hung it on one of the hooks of a wall mounted coat rack in the mudroom.

"That's the second time this month, isn't it?" Trevor asked.

"Third, sir," Emily replied as she returned to where Trevor was standing and reached for the baby.

"Here, I'll take him now. He missed his morning bottle and needs a diaper change."

"I thought my little slugger smelled a little ripe," Trevor said, grimacing as handed Eli back to her.

"I didn't expect you to be here when we got back," she continued. "I'm guessing you're back because of the storm?"

"You guessed right," Trevor answered. "I did have enough time to find some major storm damage to the fencing though. A large portion of the northern fence line will need to be repaired or in worst case replaced."

THE HIGH COUNTRY

"That'll take time," she replied.

"A week, possibly two. I just need these storms to let up. I don't need any more trees falling on the good sections of that fence. It's already bad enough," Trevor responded.

A loud clap of thunder rumbled the windows and startled the baby and he began crying. Emily gently rocked and rubbed his back as she left Trevor and headed toward the nursery. She couldn't help but notice the unmistakable odor coming from Eli's diaper.

Yep, she thought, *definitely the diaper change comes first.*

After changing Eli and giving him his morning meal and bottle she put him in his crib and went to Caroline's room to clean and change her linens. She pulled the comforter from the bed and three crumpled pieces of papers drifted to the floor.

Thinking nothing of it she simply put the papers into her pocket for inspection and disposal later. She replaced the sheets and was putting the comforter back into place when the phone rang.

She walked into the hall and down to the master bedroom for the extension line. Since the funeral Trevor had stopped answering the phone. He couldn't handle any more condolences. She picked the receiver up on the second ring.

"Brigston Residence," she said.

"Hello," said the caller, "May I speak with either Mr. or Mrs. Brigston please?"

"May I tell Mr. Brigston who's calling please?" asked Emily.

"This is Molly Swanson. I am Caroline's new teacher," Molly replied.

"Just a moment," Emily replied as she laid down the receiver and went to find Trevor.

She found him in the den staring out of the bay window sipping a cup of coffee. He turned as he heard her enter the room.

"Who was that on the phone?" he asked.

"Caroline's teacher," replied Emily. "She is asking to speak with you. She's still on the line."

"Oh, really," said Trevor raising an eyebrow. "Did she say what it was about?"

"No sir, she didn't and sorry, but I didn't ask," Emily said as she left the room.

Trevor picked up the receiver of the phone on the table and said, "Trevor Brigston, how can I help you?"

"Mr. Brigston, This is Molly Swanson. I am Caroline's new teacher."

"What happened to Mrs. Whitworth?" Trevor asked.

"I thought Caroline would have told you. She retired just before Christmas," she replied.

"No, I had no idea. Again, how can I help you?" he asked.

"Well, to tell you the truth, I'm a little concerned about Caroline," she replied.

"How so?" Trevor asked.

"Didn't you get the notes I sent home with her?" Molly asked.

"No, I haven't seen any notes."

"I thought as much when she didn't return them. She was supposed to have them signed by a parent and return them to me."

"Can you fill me in on what the notes were in reference to?" Trevor asked.

"I don't want to discuss this over the phone. I was hoping that you might be able to come in for a face-to-face conference at the school, say my classroom at four thirty this afternoon?" she asked.

Trevor looked at the watch on his wrist.

"I suppose that I could be there. I have to come into town anyway to order supplies for my ranch," he replied.

"Thank you, sir. I look forward to seeing you then," she said as she disconnected the call.

THE HIGH COUNTRY

"Is everything alright?" Emily asked.

"It appears that Little Bit has gotten herself into a bit of trouble at school," Trevor replied.

He had called her 'Little Bit' since the day they brought her home from the hospital.

Emily reached into her pocket and removed one of the crumpled sheets of papers that she had found in Caroline's room. She straightened it out, read it and was shocked by what she saw. It was a note from Caroline's teacher. She removed the other two to reveal that they, too, were from the school.

"I heard you mention something about notes from the teacher," Emily said.

"It appears that the teacher sent several notes home with her. Have you seen them?" he asked.

"Not until this morning," she replied as she handed Trevor the crumpled sheets.

He looked at the notes and a look of concern mixed with mild anger crossed his face.

"Where did you find these?" he asked.

"Under the covers of Caroline's bed. They fell to the floor as I was changing the sheets," Emily replied.

"Well, it looks like I'm gonna have to have me a little chat with Little Bit when she gets home. Don't tell her anything, just have her do her homework until I get back," he said as he headed to the door.

"Yes sir," was all Emily said.

Trevor walked into the office of the lumber yard and shook the rain from his coat. He looked around until he found Matthew Sloat. Matthew was his contact at the yard and was very familiar with the order history for The High Country Acres.

"Hey, Matt," Trevor said.

"Hey yourself," replied Matthew. "What can I do for you today?"

"Those storms did a number on my northern fence line. I'll need at least seventy-five four-by-four pressure treated posts. Fifteen rolls of barbed wire and twenty pounds of staple nails," Trevor replied.

"I don't have that much barbed wire in stock right now. I'll have to order it, but I can get it here in three days. The rest I have in stock. Would you like it all delivered like the last time?" Matthew asked.

"That'd be perfect. It would give me time to move the cattle and horses to the southern pasture," Trevor replied.

"I'll call you when it all comes in to finalize the delivery instructions," Matthew said.

"Fine. Just put it on the card you have on file."

"Will do," Matthew replied.

"Thanks," Trevor said as he turned and headed back through the rain to his truck. He still needed to stop by the feed store to get oats for the horses, but he was short on time. He'd have to take care of that later.

He had an appointment to keep.

CHAPTER SIX

TREVOR PULLED INTO the parking lot of Caroline's school at 3:50 p.m. Knowing that he had a little time, he sat in the truck and tried to think of questions that he would ask Caroline's teacher.

Beth had usually handled these types of things and all of this was new to him. He knew that he would have to adjust.

He was on his own now with the decision making involving his children. Of course, he had Emily for the day-to-day care, but it wasn't the same.

He shut off the ignition and got out of the truck. He pushed the button on the keyless remote and the horn beeped in response.

Adjusting his collar against the pouring rain, he headed toward the entrance of the building. Reaching the double glass doors, he put his hand on the handle and pulled.

He entered the long hallway and made his way to the classroom. Not knowing what to expect he prepared himself for the worst.

How much trouble is Caroline really in? he thought. He found the classroom and put his hand on the handle, opened the door and stepped inside.

Sitting at the desk in the front of the room was a slender, attractive young brunette. He stopped in his tracks and went back into the hallway. Looking at the number on the door to reassure himself that he was at the right room he went back inside.

He was met by a puzzled look from the woman at the desk. She had her head gently tilted to one side and was flipping a pencil against her other hand. She spoke as he came back through the door.

"Are you lost?" she asked.

"I thought I was in the wrong room. I had to take another look to make sure. You're not quite what I was expecting," Trevor replied.

"Sorry to disappoint you," she said teasingly as she got to her feet. "You must be Caroline's father."

She came around from behind the desk and extended her hand in greeting. Trevor accepted the gesture and they shook hands.

She introduced herself, "I'm Caroline's teacher, Molly Swanson."

"Trevor Brigston."

Molly motioned around the small classroom toward the various chairs in the room.

"I'd ask you to have a seat, but all of the other chairs are sized for my kindergarten students. Why don't we go into the teacher's lounge? The chairs are adult sized there," she said as gathered her notes and led the way to the lounge.

"Will Caroline's mother be joining us?" she asked as they reached the door.

"No, I'm afraid not. Caroline's mother passed away a few months back," he replied as he took a seat at the closest table. Molly took a seat across from him.

"I'm sorry, I had no idea. That would explain a lot of things," she replied.

"How's that?" he asked.

THE HIGH COUNTRY

"The notes I sent home with Caroline were addressed to both you and your wife. I told her to give them to her mother when she got home," she answered.

"So that's why she hid them from me," he said.

"You never saw them?"

"No, not until this morning when our housekeeper found them under Caroline's sheets," he replied.

"I was wondering why I never got a response. That explains one thing, but I have so much more to discuss with you."

"I'm listening," Trevor said. He put his elbow on the table and rested his chin on his fist. It nestled lightly on his index finger. His eyes caught the glint of the fluorescent lights and appeared to twinkle. He had a slight smile on his lips.

Molly couldn't help but stare at this gorgeous man seated before her. Her mind wandered for a moment and was startled when Trevor cleared his throat.

"Oh, I'm so sorry. My mind wandered for a bit. I was trying to gather my thoughts," she confided. *God he's gorgeous,* she thought.

"The reason I brought you here today is that I am concerned about Caroline. She is refusing to participate in class group sessions to the point she has started lashing out if I even suggest it," she said.

"Her grades are starting to suffer and I'm afraid that if she doesn't turn herself around I won't have any choice but to hold her back."

"Has there been a progress report that I've missed somewhere? Aren't they supposed to go out every few weeks?" Trevor asked.

"They are scheduled to be sent out next week. I wanted to tell you so that you'd know to be expecting it," she answered.

"Caroline has also been acting up in class. She has become sort of a bully. Teasing and taunting the other children. She even struck a girl who has been one of her closest friends since the beginning of the school year. Just last week, she stood up on a table and started twirling around to the point her dress was flying up and showing her panties," she continued.

"Why haven't you called me about this before?" asked Trevor.

"I thought that Caroline had given you my notes and I was waiting on your response. After the second note had no reply, I started getting suspicious and questioned her about it. She assured me that she gave them to you. She also told me that you were 'too busy' to get back to me."

"Now I know that was not the case," she continued.

"I will take care of this," he assured her. "I had no idea that any of this was happening. And I can promise you that it won't happen again."

He stood and offered his hand to her again and she shook it.

"I will call you if anything else happens seeing that the notes didn't work," she promised.

"Please do," he said. "I want to thank you for taking the time to speak with me today, but please keep in mind that Caroline has been through a lot lately."

"Now that I'm aware of her situation I will try to find the time to sit down and work more with her one-on-one," she promised.

"That might be helpful for her. Thank you," he said.

"Don't mention it," she replied as she led him back to the main entrance.

As Trevor walked back to his truck, he thought of his pending talk with Caroline. He couldn't let her know that he had already talked with her teacher.

He was going to give her a chance to come clean and, hopefully, redeem herself.

Pulling out onto the main highway, he headed home.

He had his work cut out for him, in more ways than one.

But at least the rain had stopped.

Caroline was sitting at the kitchen table working on her homework as Emily prepared their evening meal. Eli was in his high chair nibbling on an animal cracker.

"I don't understand this part," Caroline said.

"Let me take a look at it," replied Emily as she looked over the child's shoulder.

Before Emily could finish reading the assignment, they heard the crunching of gravel from the driveway.

"Daddy!" Caroline shouted as she ran toward the door.

As Trevor stepped through the door he scooped her up into her arms and held her tight.

"What have you been up to today?" he asked.

"Just doing my homework. Emily was helping me when you came home," she replied.

"Emily, would you mind leaving us alone for a little while?" Trevor asked.

"Not at all, sir," Emily replied. She picked Eli up from his high chair and headed toward the stairs. "This little man needs a fresh diaper anyway."

When they were alone Trevor looked at Caroline and asked, "Do you have something that you need to tell me?" He put her down and looked her in the eyes.

Caroline thought for a minute and shook her head.

"No? Nothing that might have happened at school?" he quizzed.

Caroline's smile vanished and was replaced with a look of dread. She thought for a few seconds more before she added.

"I don't think so," she said.

"Okay then, I'll get right to the point. Did your teacher send anything home with you that I needed to see?" he asked

"Uh oh," she said as she dropped her head.

"I thought so," Trevor said. "Mind telling me the truth now?"

"Ms. Swanson told me I had to give you some papers, but she can't tell me what to do. She isn't Mommy," Caroline protested.

"Is that what this is about?" Trevor asked. "Honey, she isn't trying to be your Mommy. She's trying to be your teacher. It's her job to instruct you in the things that you need to learn."

"Well, I don't like it. She's mean to me," Caroline answered.

"I had a talk with Ms. Swanson this afternoon and we discussed your behavior in her class. Do you want to explain to me why she thinks you are being a bully? Pushing and hitting other kids? Not doing your assignments?" Trevor asked.

"Those kids deserved it. They were saying mean things about Mommy," Caroline replied.

"No one deserves to be pushed or punched for any reason," Trevor scolded.

"But…" Caroline started to protest.

"But nothing," Trevor stopped her. "You will go in Monday morning and you will apologize to those kids and Ms. Swanson. You will also bring your classroom assignments up to date and turn them in. Until you do, there will be no more trail rides for you on Chocolate. Do you understand?"

"That's not fair!" Caroline squealed.

"It's not open for any further discussion. You are to stay away from the barn and your horse until further notice. And in the future, I suggest that you give me all of the notes that your teacher gives to you. I don't want us to ever have to talk about this again. Do I make myself clear?" Trevor admonished.

"Yes sir," Caroline said.

THE HIGH COUNTRY

"Now I suggest you go to your room and get busy. I want you to clean your room before dinner. Then I'll help with your homework," Trevor said.

Caroline hung her head as she stood and headed toward the stairs. She wanted to say something else but stopped herself. It would be best if she didn't.

She was in enough trouble already.

CHAPTER SEVEN

EMILY GATHERED THE plates from the cupboard and placed them on the cloth mats at each of their seats at the dinner table. She placed the napkin wrapped silverware next to each plate and went back into the kitchen.

She returned with a steaming bowl filled with her special recipe pot roast. After placing it in the center of the table, she went back for the rest of their meal. Sweet corn on the cob, Italian green beans and fresh baked dinner rolls.

Emily went to the den and found Trevor staring at the computer monitor sitting on the desk.

"Your dinner is ready sir," she said. "Shall I go get the children?"

"Caroline is probably still sulking in her room. She might come down easier if you go. I'll go get Eli," he replied.

Emily got to Caroline's room and, as a courtesy, knocked on the door.

"Anyone home?" she asked.

"No one but us chickens," came Caroline's reply. She always said the same thing every time Emily knocked on her door.

THE HIGH COUNTRY

Emily opened the door and stepped inside. "Your dinner is ready, are you ready for it?" she asked.

"I guess so. Is Daddy still mad?" she asked.

"I don't think so. He's coming up to the nursery to get your brother. He seemed fine to me," Emily replied.

"Good. I don't like it when he's mad at me," Caroline said.

"Neither do I," replied Emily. "Shall we go downstairs now?"

"Yep, I'm starving," the child said.

"Good, because I made your favorite," Emily said.

Caroline looked up at her and smiled as she took Emily's hand and headed downstairs.

Emily walked over to where Trevor stood. She took Eli from him and sat him down in his high chair.

"Don't mind me, you guys go ahead. I have to get this little man his dinner," she said as she secured a bib around Eli's neck.

She went to the kitchen cupboard, retrieved two glass jars of baby food and returned to the dining room table. Eli saw the jars in Emily's hand and started kicking excitedly.

"Thought you might be hungry," she said to the baby.

"Oh, I almost forgot," Emily said as she spooned the first of the creamed carrots into Eli's open mouth.

"The lumber yard called this morning and said your order is ready. They said that they could deliver it in the morning. I told them to put it under the overhang on the south side of the barn, out of the weather."

Trevor had just put a forkful of green beans into his mouth, so he simply nodded. After he swallowed, he looked at Emily.

"That's a good idea, what with the afternoon thunderstorms that keep cropping up," he said. "Logan and I can get to work on moving some of it up to the fence line tomorrow afternoon. Thanks."

"Not a problem," she said as she wiped Eli's face.

"Caroline, if you've finished your dinner, it's time for your bath. Go upstairs and I'll be up in a minute to run the water," Emily continued.

"I've got it. You take care of Eli. It's been a while since I have spent quality time with my daughter." He turned to his daughter with a challenge

"Race you upstairs."

Caroline giggled as she stood and ran toward the stairs. Trevor let her have a good head start before heading in that direction.

Halfway up the stairs he scooped her up and hugged her tight.

"Daddy, that's cheating. I was winning," Caroline complained.

"You're always a winner in my book," Trevor answered as he kissed her cheek. He put her down on the cold ceramic tiles of the bathroom floor.

As her feet touched the tiles she said, "It's cold in here."

Trevor reached out and switched on the portable heater and adjusted the temperature. The warm air immediately began to fill the small room.

"How's that?" he asked as he reached for the faucet. Turning on the taps, he adjusted the temperature of the water, he stopped the drain and let the water run.

When it had gotten to an adequate depth, he turned off the flow and helped his daughter get undressed and into the tub.

"Emily usually washes my hair first. That way the water is not too soapy," Caroline instructed.

"Yes, ma'am," Trevor replied as he wet and lathered her long locks. Caroline giggled as the water trickled down her back. She tilted her head back so that the water wouldn't get into her eyes.

"Daddy, will you dry my hair and then read me a bedtime story?" Caroline asked.

THE HIGH COUNTRY

"Sure," he replied. "You pick out the book and I'll read it to you."

It had been a while since he had had this much quality time with his daughter. He wasn't going to waste any more time away from her or his son.

They were now his entire world and it was his job to nurture and protect them. In his grief, he had forgotten that one factor.

He wouldn't be forgetting that again.

Dressed in fresh pajamas and smelling of baby shampoo, Caroline burst into her room and ran to her bookshelf. She picked out her favorite storybook. It was the one that Beth had always read from.

"This one Daddy," she said. She held up a book of Aesop's fables. "I like this one."

"Sure thing, Little Bit," he replied as he opened the book and selected a story. He began reading aloud to the child, but before he could finish the story Caroline was sound asleep.

He softly closed the book and tiptoed to the door. Turning out the light before he left, he couldn't help but stare at his sleeping daughter. She looked so much like her mother. Beth was beautiful, but Caroline is lovely in her own special way.

He thought, *I need to remind her of that every day. Of how special she is to me.*

CHAPTER EIGHT

THE LUMBER TRUCK was pulling into the driveway as Trevor was heading out of the barn from feeding the horses.

Matthew stopped the truck and shut off the ignition when he saw Trevor. He got out and walked over to him.

"I wasn't sure if I was going to be able to catch you," Matthew said. "You still want me to put it under the overhang?"

"Would it be possible for you to take it on up to the fence line? I was going to use my tractor to pull the lumber on my trailer, but I couldn't get it running this morning. Your truck has sufficient clearance that it should make the trip without too much trouble," Trevor said.

"Sure thing, there is just one problem," Matthew answered. "I don't know exactly where your fence line is."

"Give me a few minutes. I need to give my housekeeper a message for Logan when he gets back. Then, I'll saddle up one of my horses and lead the way," Trevor replied.

Trevor walked into the kitchen where Emily was busy washing the lunch dishes. She looked around as she heard the door opening.

THE HIGH COUNTRY

"Emily can you give Logan a message for me?" he asked.

"Yes, sir," she replied.

"The lumber is here, and Matthew is delivering it up to the fence line. Logan needs to join me there as soon as he gets back. He can take one of the other horses," Trevor said.

"I'll tell him," Emily promised.

"Thanks," Trevor said as he went back outside. He went to the barn and removed a bridle. Walking over to one of the stalls, he opened the door and went inside.

"Hello girl," he said as he patted the horse's neck.

The horse snorted at him and shook her head. He placed the bit of the bridle between the horse's teeth, looped and secured the harness over her ears, then took a saddle and blanket from the tack rack and threw it over the back of the horse.

Chocolate shifted as he tightened the saddle strap across her stomach. She let out a loud snort as he finished cinching the buckle. He led her out of the barn and walked over to Matthew's truck.

"Ready?" he asked Matthew as he put his foot into the stirrup and hefted himself into the saddle.

"Lead on," Matthew replied as he started his engine and put the truck in gear.

Trevor softly nudged Chocolate's sides and turned her toward the pasture. Matthew pulled out and followed Trevor's lead.

Matthew and Trevor had just started to off load the lumber when Logan rode up on horseback. He dismounted, tied the reins to an undamaged section of the fencing and jumped into the back of the truck to help with the task at hand.

They were finishing with the last of the lumber when a piercing scream filled the still air. All three looked toward the origin of the sound. They were shocked to see a woman on horseback who continued to scream as she tried to stop her horse. Her efforts proved unsuccessful and the horse continued to charge and snort, oblivious to her feeble attempts with the reins.

Trevor jumped from the back of the truck and ran to Chocolate. He was astride the animal in one leap and nudged the horse into motion.

Leading her through a broken section of the fencing, he heeled the horse's sides to get her to a faster pace.

It took several minutes before Chocolate was alongside the terrified rider. Trevor reached out and wrapped his left arm around the waist of the woman and pulled her off her horse and onto his. As he was pulling the reins to slow Chocolate's pace, the woman looked up at Trevor.

"Oh, it's you," was all she said as she went limp in his arms. Trevor headed Chocolate back to the ranch house, with Logan and Matthew not far behind.

Trevor held onto the reins with one hand as he supported the woman's limp form with the other. His arm was starting to tremble and throb from the additional strain when the ranch house came into view.

He carefully dismounted as he reached the back porch, supporting the woman's limp form and easing her into his arms from the saddle.

Emily, seeing him approach, ran to the door and held it open wide for them to enter the house.

"Put her on the sofa over there," Emily instructed. "I'll get a cold cloth for her forehead. Then you can fill me in on exactly what happened."

Emily returned with the cloth and placed it carefully across the woman's brow.

"Well... I'm waiting," Emily said, slightly scolding.

"We were unloading the lumber when we heard her scream and saw her horse running at full steam and she couldn't stop it. Why it was running that hard is something you'll have to ask her," Trevor replied as he pointed to the woman.

THE HIGH COUNTRY

No sooner than that statement was spoken, the woman started to stir and opened her eyes.

"Welcome back young lady. It was touch and go there for a while," Trevor said with a grin.

"Emily, allow me to introduce you to our guest. I'd like you to meet Ms. Molly Swanson, Caroline's teacher."

CHAPTER NINE

MOLLY LOOKED AROUND and in her confused state uttered, "What are you doing here?"

"I live here," Trevor answered.

Molly blinked to focus her eyes as she looked around the room. She realized that she didn't recognize anything in the room. Well… there was *one* exception. That would be the cowboy looking down at her.

"Oh, then I guess the better question would be, what am I doing here?" she asked sheepishly.

"Well, I can tell you the story of *how* you got here. But I'm afraid you're gonna have to tell *us* exactly what happened… and why," Trevor answered her.

Molly rubbed her forehead and the cloth fell to the floor. She reached for it, but Emily beat her to it. Scooping it up she scolded Molly.

"You'd best be still now! Doc Barnett is on his way."

"*You called a doctor?*" Molly asked incredulously.

"Well…sorta. Doc Barnett is the vet who treats our livestock. He's the only doctor I know of that still makes house calls," Emily said as she turned and hurried toward the kitchen.

THE HIGH COUNTRY

She couldn't help but feel Trevor's hardened stare on her back as she left the room. She didn't dare return the glance. *Nope, not on your life,* she thought.

"*A vet?*" Molly asked.

"Well actually, he *was* a regular M.D. before he went to Veterinary school at the University of Colorado," Trevor assured her. "He got tired of human bedside manners. Found that animals were a lot more cooperative. Although right now, he thinks you're my prize heifer about to give birth."

"Oh, that makes me feel so much better!" she said as she threw her legs over the edge of the sofa and sat up.

There was a knock at the door and Trevor put his hand up and motioned for her to sit still. He went to open it and stepped aside so their guest could enter.

"I tried to find you out in the barn. Couldn't find that cow of yours that's about to calf either. Mind telling me what's really going on here?" Doctor Barnett asked skeptically. One of his eyebrows was raised as he looked at Trevor.

"Sorry for the slight deception Doc," Trevor said. "I thought you might not come all the way out here if you knew it was a *human* patient."

"And you would have been right," the doctor retorted. "But now that I'm here, what have we got?"

"She's in here," Trevor said as he led the doctor over to Molly.

"Hello, I'm Doctor Henry Barnett, but most people just call me 'Doc'," the doctor said as he extended his hand to Molly. Molly took the offered hand and shook it.

"I'm Molly... Molly Swanson." Doc sat down on the sofa beside Molly to take a good look at her face. More specifically, her eyes.

"Can you tell me what happened?" Doc asked.

"She passed out and…" Trevor started.

The doctor interrupted him with, "Can you please let *her* answer my questions?"

"Oh... yeah... sure... sorry," Trevor sputtered.

"Now that we've got *that* clarified, what happened?" he asked as he turned back toward Molly.

"I was riding my horse on the farm where I board her. Something must have spooked her because she reared up and took off running. I couldn't stop her. Mr. Brigston just happened to be at the right place at the right time to help me," she answered.

"I guess I didn't really have the chance to say thank you, so, thank you." She looked from the doctor over to Trevor and back again.

"I must have passed out, like he said. The next thing I remember is waking up here," she continued.

"Did you hit your head on anything?" Doc asked.

"Not that I know of," she said as she looked over at Trevor questioningly.

"I didn't see you hit your head on anything," Trevor said. "Unless you hit it before I saw you."

The doctor was shining his flashlight in her eyes as she answered.

"Then, no, I guess I didn't."

"How long was she unconscious?" Doc asked Trevor.

"About ten minutes," Trevor replied.

"Your pupils are equal and reactive. Your vital signs are good. No bruises or contusions that I can see. I think you just had a minor shock to your system. It just temporarily had to shut down to reboot, so to speak. You should be just fine," Doc said as he patted her knee.

"Thank you, doctor," Molly said.

The doctor stood, and he and Trevor headed toward the front door. As they got closer to the door Trevor leaned over and said softly to the doctor.

"Thank you, Doc, just send me the bill and I'll pay it."

"I'll do that. If I may say so," the doctor responded in a hushed tone. "You've got yourself a fine catch there son.

THE HIGH COUNTRY

Might not want to let her get away." Doc gave him a sly wink.

Trevor grinned as the doctor opened the door and Trevor walked him to his truck.

As the doctor opened the door he turned and said to Trevor, "Look for my bill. It will say 'for treatment of filly'."

Trevor couldn't help but smile as he walked back toward the house.

Molly was still sitting in the same spot on the sofa when he came back into the room. She looked up when he got closer.

"OH MY GOD!" she shouted, jumping up and starting toward the door. "I've got to go back out and find my horse. I don't have much time to look before it gets dark."

"Calm yourself," Trevor soothed. "Logan brought her in while I was outside with Doc. She's in the barn and will be safe there for tonight. I'll take you to your car and you can come back for her tomorrow. Deal?"

"Deal," Molly said. "I don't know how I'll ever thank you,"

"Don't mention it," he replied as he picked up his keys. "You ready?"

"I guess I am," was all she said.

Even though the two ranches border each other, the ride from High Country Acres to the Twin Eagles Ranch usually took about fifteen minutes. During the first seven of them there was an awkward silence between them. Molly was the first to speak.

"I've got it!" she blurted.

"Got what?" Trevor asked. He was a little startled by her outburst and it showed in the tone of his voice.

"Oh, sorry, I didn't mean to startle you. It's just that I've thought of a way to thank you for helping me," she relied.

"I thought I told you that that wasn't necessary?" he said as he glanced over at her.

"I know you did, but I want to do it and it isn't much. I want you to come to my house for dinner on Saturday night and I won't take no for an answer," she stated emphatically.

"Dinner?" he asked.

"I want to fix you one of my grandmother's recipes," she replied.

"Well who am I to argue with Granny?" he conceded as he pulled up to the ranch house of the Twin Eagles ranch.

"Good," she said. She scribbled something hastily on a piece of paper. "Here are the directions, 7:00 p.m. sharp."

She handed him the slip of paper and got out of the truck. Trevor watched as she went to the front door and rang the bell. A few minutes later he put the truck into reverse as the door opened and she stepped inside.

No sooner than she crossed the threshold, Clifford Gordon grabbed her in a strong embrace.

"*Girl, where have you been*? I have the boys out on horseback looking for you. You should've been back hours ago," he blurted as he held her tight.

"I'm sorry that I worried you Uncle Cliff, but I'll explain everything on one condition," she promised as she returned the hug.

"Condition?" he asked, releasing her from the embrace and looking into her eyes.

"That you let me borrow one of your guestrooms for the night," she replied.

"And here I thought it was something major. I've already had Ruth freshen up one of the extra rooms for ya."

"Thanks," she said as she headed toward the hallway and an awaiting warm bed.

"What about my explanation?" he called after her.

"In the morning," she promised loudly as she opened the bedroom door and stepped inside.

Well, at least she's back in one piece, he thought. He picked up his phone and called Luke, his cowhand and search team leader. Luke answered on the first ring.

THE HIGH COUNTRY

"You guys can call off the search. She turned up here about five minutes ago," he said into the receiver, not waiting for a greeting.

After listening for a moment, he said, "I don't have anything to tell you at the moment. She promised to give me an explanation in the morning. Thanks for helping. You guys can go on home from there."

Cliff pushed the end button and ran his fingers through his gray hair.

She had better have a damn good reason why she's so late, he thought as he headed toward his room.

CHAPTER TEN

MOLLY WAS AWAKENED by the glare of the morning sun shining through the slats of the window blinds.

Great, she thought, *I had to pick the room on the east side of the house.*

She threw back the covers and rolled out of bed. Smelling the aroma of freshly brewed coffee, she dressed quickly and hurried downstairs.

She found Cliff in the kitchen standing in front of the coffee pot. He had the full pot in one hand and a large mug in the other. He turned around when he heard her footsteps.

"I'm *still* waiting for that explanation you promised me *last night,*" he scolded as he filled the mug and held it out to her.

"Thanks," she said as she took the offered steaming brew.

"Oh, and I called my sister last night," Cliff said. Molly's face lost its color with those words.

"What did you go and do a thing like that for?" Molly asked.

THE HIGH COUNTRY

"You were missing and she's your mother. Why shouldn't I call her?" he calmly replied.

"I know…it's just…you know how she gets," Molly replied. "She never got over the fact that I moved to Wyoming. She's still angry about it and keeps trying to talk me into moving back home. We had a big argument about it."

"You aren't telling me anything I don't already know but she's on her way. She'll be here tonight," Cliff admitted.

"And I won't be here," Molly retorted. "Because I have to go retrieve Lucy. Can you give me a lift to The High Country?"

"Why do you need to go there?" Cliff asked as his wife Ruth entered the room.

"Where?" asked Ruth.

"The High Country," answered Molly. "That's where Lucy is."

"That's where you were all this time?" asked Ruth incredulously.

"It's not like that Aunt Ruth," responded Molly. "I was riding Lucy around in the pasture like I usually do when something spooked her. Next thing I knew she was bolting across the pasture at full steam and I couldn't stop her."

"Oh, my word!" gasped Ruth as she placed her hand over her mouth.

"How did you get to High Country?" Cliff asked.

"I guess Mr. Brigston was just in the right place at the right time," Molly replied. "He was on the property line and pulled me off Lucy. I felt my butt hit his saddle right before I passed out."

"You what?" Ruth asked.

"Will you stop doing that Ruth. Let her tell us what happened?" Cliff scolded.

Ruth just blushed, hushed and leaned back against the kitchen counter.

"I must have been out for quite a while because when I came to, a doctor was already on the way," Molly continued.

"A doctor?" asked Ruth. Cliff gave her a glaring look and she didn't say anything else.

"After the doctor left, Mr. Brigston gave me a ride back here. Lucy is still in his barn. Now can I have that lift or not?" Molly continued.

"What's your hurry?" Cliff asked. "I plan on finishing my coffee first." He sipped his coffee leisurely while Molly paced impatiently.

When he finished, he sat the empty mug on the counter.

"I'm ready now," he said as he picked up his keys. "But I just need to hitch up the horse trailer."

"Don't bother," she said. "I'll just ride her back. She should be fine now."

"Suit yourself," Cliff replied. "Makes no difference to me."

Trevor was walking out to the barn to give the horses their morning oats when he heard the crunch of gravel in the driveway. He turned and saw Cliff Gordon's truck approaching. It was surrounded by a billowing cloud of dust. The dust settled though as Cliff pulled up alongside Trevor's F-150.

Trevor turned and walked over to where the truck was parked. Cliff rolled down his window.

"Morning, Cliff," Trevor said. "You're out awfully early."

"Molly wouldn't hush until we came back for Lucy," Cliff replied.

"She's fine," Trevor answered. "I was just about to feed her and the other horses."

Molly got out of the truck and looked toward the barn.

"I can help you with that," Molly offered.

"Sure thing, follow me," Trevor instructed as he led the way.

"Thanks for the ride Uncle Cliff," Molly called out to Cliff. "I'll see you in a little while."

"Well if something happens *this time*, at least I know where to start looking," he said as he put the truck into reverse and turned it around.

"All I ask is that you be careful," Cliff continued.

"You worry too much," Molly scolded.

"After last night, I have good reason to," Cliff chided as he pulled the truck into gear and headed back to Twin Eagles.

Trevor looked at Molly and raised an eyebrow and asked, "Uncle?"

"Yes," Molly answered. "My mother is Cliff's sister."

"Small world isn't it?" Trevor kidded.

"And getting smaller by the minute," Molly said under her breath.

Trevor pretended not to hear as they entered the storage area where he kept the oats and hay. The door to the storage stall squeaked as Trevor opened it and they stepped inside.

"I've been meaning to oil that, but I keep forgetting about it until it squeaks again," Trevor said. He walked over to a large, round metal drum and removed the lid.

Removing three buckets from the pegs on the slats of the stall he started scooping the oats from the drum into each of the buckets. He handed a bucket to Molly. Her hand brushed his as she took it. A slight tingle ran down her spine. It felt a little like static electricity.

"Thought *you* might like to feed your horse. What's her name?" Trevor asked.

Shaking off the tingle she'd just felt, she answered, "Her name is Lucy."

She took the bucket to Lucy's stall and dumped the contents into the feeding trough in the stall. Lucy had kicked over her water bucket, making a mud puddle in the corner of the stall.

"Look what you did," she scolded. "Guess you weren't thirsty." The horse nodded her head as if agreeing with her.

Still, Molly refilled the bucket and replaced it in the stall.

"When she's finished eating, I'll saddle her up and be on my way," she said.

"She's having her breakfast, but have you had yours?" Trevor asked.

"Not yet," she replied. "I'll get something when I get back to Twin Eagles."

"Nonsense," Trevor admonished. "Emily always cooks enough for an army. You're welcome to eat with us."

"I'd like that," she replied, blushing just a little. "If you're sure it's not too much trouble."

"To tell you the truth, I'd enjoy the company," Trevor admitted.

Maybe there might have been something to that shiver after all, she thought.

CHAPTER ELEVEN

AFTER BREAKFAST TREVOR and Molly went back to the barn. As Molly was saddling up Lucy she looked over to the next stall. Trevor was doing the same to one of his horses, a mustang named Maverick.

"I thought I'd ride with you as far as my fence line. Unfortunately, you're on your own after that. Maybe nothing will spook her this time," Trevor said as he tightened the cinch on the saddle. Maverick gave a slight cough in protest.

"Sorry boy," Trevor soothed as he patted the horse's neck.

"Are you ready?" he asked Molly.

Molly placed her foot into the stirrup and grabbing the saddle horn she hefted herself into the saddle.

"I am now," she answered. "Let's go." She nudged Lucy's sides to get her moving.

"Feel like a race?" she challenged.

"I think we'd better take it slow for now," Trevor replied.

"You seemed to have forgotten," she teased as she kicked Lucy's side to get her into a run. "I have a class to teach in a little over an hour."

"In that case you're on," answered Trevor as he nudged Maverick's sides as well. Both horses reached a full gallop over the rugged terrain, Trevor having a slight lead.

Molly leaned into Lucy's neck and whispered to the horse, "We can't let the men win girl. Give it all you've got." At this Lucy lunged and gained a little on Maverick.

"Oh, no you don't," Trevor challenged as he urged Maverick to increase his speed as well. By the time they reached the fence line Trevor led by a length and a half.

Just when he thought his win was in the bag, Trevor heard a sharp shriek of "Heeyaah!"

Molly flashed by him in a cloud of dust and across the finish line which was an opening in a section of damaged fence.

She leaned back in the saddle and yanked the reins, hard.

"Whoa girl!" Molly shouted as she pulled the reins closer to her chest. Lucy's hooves kicked up a larger cloud of dust as the horse attempted to comply with Molly's request.

When the horse slowed, Molly tightened her hold on the reins and leaned to the right. The rein touched the left side of Lucy's neck and the effect was immediate.

The horse turned completely around to the right and came to a stop as Molly pulled back on the harness.

Trevor was waving his hand in front of his face, coughing and spitting profusely from her churned up dust as he tugged on Maverick's reins to stop him.

"Where were you hiding that?" Trevor asked, still coughing.

"I'll fill you in Saturday night," she promised. "That is…if we're still on for Saturday. Right now, I have to get home, shower, change and head to work."

"Then I'll see you on Saturday," he replied.

"Until Saturday," she said as she turned Lucy toward Twin Eagles. He was smiling broadly as he dismounted Maverick and tied him to one of the undamaged posts.

THE HIGH COUNTRY

Someone is going to have their hands full with her, he thought as he picked up a set of post hole diggers.

He lifted them high over his head, opened the handles wide and thrust them into the hardened soil with a loud thud. He had just gotten the hole to the right depth when he heard a noise behind him. He turned to see Logan dismounting his horse and tying its reins to a low hanging tree branch.

"I know you said to meet you up here at 9:00 a.m.," Logan said. "But I thought I'd come up early and get a head start."

"I did say that, yes," Trevor replied. "But that was before Ms. Swanson decided she wanted to ride back to Twin Eagles. I rode with her as far as the fence line."

"I hope there were no problems this time," Logan said.

"Not really other than I challenged her to a race and lost," Trevor replied.

"How could you lose a race on Maverick?" Logan asked.

"Beats me," Trevor answered. "She's supposed to explain everything to me this Saturday. We have dinner plans."

"Well don't that beat all?" said Logan as he picked up a fence post and placed it in the hole. Reaching for the shovel, he started filling the hole.

"One down," said Logan as he wiped his brow. "Only a hundred more to go."

Cliff Gordon looked up as the front door opened and his niece entered the room. She walked over and kissed him on the cheek.

"I have to hurry," she said as she started down the hallway. "Or I'm going to be late for school."

"But you're the teacher," Cliff replied.

"I know, right," Molly answered from the doorway of the guest room.

Molly came back into the living room with her purse and keys.

"Where's Aunt Ruth?" she asked.

"She went to the market," Cliff replied.

"Tell her that I'm sorry I missed her and that I'll call her later," Molly said.

"Will do," replied Cliff as he watched her walk out of the door.

CHAPTER TWELVE

MOLLY WALKED INTO her classroom and wasn't surprised that the room was in total chaos. Two boys were at the dry erase board and had written graffiti all over its surface.

Two girls were sitting in the middle of the floor braiding a third girl's hair.

One boy had the scoop from a jar of paste in his mouth. She was only five minutes late from the beginning of class bell.

"WHAT IS GOING ON IN HERE?" she shouted above the din.

The entire room quieted and looked up at her, puzzled.

"Landon, give me that jar. You know better than to eat this. I've told you several times this is NOT food," she admonished.

She looked at the ingredients on the jar. Nothing that could hurt him as the label listed the contents as non-toxic. Still she would need to send a note home to his parents informing them of this incident.

"Jonah, you and Tristen get that board cleaned off," she instructed as she handed them both an eraser.

"Yes ma'am," replied Tristen as he and Jonah started rubbing the erasers on the board, removing the evidence of their mischief.

She sat down at her desk and took out the lesson plan that she had prepared for the class. Jonah and Tristen finished cleaning the board and returned to their seats.

This is going to be the longest week on record, Molly thought.

All she could think about was the coming weekend and her date with Trevor.

But first she had to make it through the week.

Trevor was having trouble with the last section of the barbed wire fencing and Logan stepped over to help.

As he pulled the wire to the desired spot, Trevor was ready with the nail brad. As he hammered the brad into place Logan spoke up.

"Are you sure you're ready to start dating again?" he asked.

Trevor looked at him, slightly taken aback.

"I'm not '*dating again*'," he said. "It's just a dinner to thank me for helping her."

"That's what you think, what about what *she* thinks?" asked Logan.

"*It's not a date! I don't care what she thinks!*" Trevor stated emphatically.

"Okay, okay. I hear you," Logan conceded. "Hey, if we're through here, can we go back to the house? I'm starving for some of Emily's home cooking."

"I'm a little hungry too," Trevor admitted. "After lunch, we can get started on that other section of fencing."

He was just glad that Logan had changed the subject of the conversation. He had been trying to convince himself that

THE HIGH COUNTRY

it was just a casual dinner with Caroline's teacher, nothing more.

What does she think about the dinner? he thought.

He decided to give her a call later to test those waters.

Trevor and Logan collected some of the tools and cinched the ones that would not fit into the bags to the side of the saddle. The others they would pick up later.

He and Logan mounted their horses and headed back to the ranch house. Trevor was thinking about the stew that Emily had made for last night's dinner and he hoped there was some left over.

When they reached the barn, they led the horses into their stalls and gave them some fresh water. Securing the doors to the stalls, they headed to the house.

As they stepped into the mud room, the aroma wafting from the kitchen intensified their hunger. Emily was standing at the stove stirring a pot simmering over one of the burners.

"Smells great Emily," said Trevor as he walked up behind her and looked over her shoulder into the pot. The stew was bubbling, and Emily gave it another stir.

"You liked it so much last night I thought I'd reheat it. I hope you don't mind leftovers," Emily said.

"As a matter of fact, I was craving your stew," Trevor admitted. He looked around the room and asked, "Where's Eli?"

"I put him down for his nap about a half hour ago. He was getting too irritable and cranky," Emily replied.

"Lunch is ready," Emily said as she tapped the spoon on the side of the pot. "Just get a bowl and help yourself." She laid the spoon on the counter and wiped her hands on her apron.

"You're not having any?" Logan asked.

"I'll get some later, that is if you two leave any for me," Emily said with a smile.

"I make no promises," Trevor said. He opened a cabinet and removed two bowls, handing one to Logan.

Emily opened the oven and removed a fresh pan of cornbread and brushed its steaming surface with melted butter. She cut the cornbread into squares and brushed the remaining butter over the cuts allowing the golden liquid to seep into the cracks of the bread.

She took the pan to the table and put it on a cast iron trivet shaped like a horseshoe.

"You guys eat up," Emily said as she removed her apron and laid it over the back of one of the chairs. "I think I'll go check on Eli," she said over her shoulder as she left the room.

"I gonna need to run into town this afternoon," Trevor said. "I used the last of the brad nails before we broke for lunch."

Logan wiped his mouth with a cloth napkin and placed it on the table beside his bowl.

"I'll go back up to the fence line and check out the remaining bad sections. Then I'll start digging a few more holes for the new posts and try to have them ready for when you get back," Logan responded as he rose from his chair.

"Sounds like a plan," said Trevor. "I'll just meet you up there, but can you do me a favor?"

"Name it," Logan replied.

"Can you take that other set of wire cutters with you? The ones we were using are getting dull and I don't have time to sharpen them right now," Trevor answered.

"You've got it," Logan replied.

Molly was headed to the teacher's lounge when her cell phone chirped from her pocket. She pushed the mute button on the side of the device to silence it, absently deciding to return the call later.

Pushing the door to the lounge open, she hurried over to the refrigerator and removed a small plastic container.

She lifted the edge of the lid and popped the small container into the microwave. As the aroma of leftover spaghetti filled the small room, she pulled her phone from her pocket and looked at its display.

According to the text on the screen, she had a voicemail message. Listening to it she couldn't help but smile.

It was from Trevor.

"I just thought I'd call and see if you needed me to bring anything for the dinner on Saturday. You're probably a little busy right now so I'll try back a little later," the recording said.

She forgot all about her lunch and her hunger as her heart literally skipped a beat.

She immediately pushed the button to return the call.

CHAPTER THIRTEEN

THE CALL FROM Trevor had lifted her spirits enough to make it through the rest of her week. She was so thankful when Friday finally arrived. After having to deal with a paste eater, the graffiti artist duo and crayon throwing children this week, she was desperate for an intelligent adult conversation.

Her dinner with Trevor would provide just that. She was going to stop at the grocery store on her way home to get two thick, prime cut ribeye steaks to cook on her small Weber charcoal grill. Thinking about the taste of those steaks made her mouth water.

Molly decided that she was going to make her grandmother's chocolate sheet cake for their dessert. She needed to get the ingredients for that as well.

She kept watching the seconds tick away on the clock above the classroom door until finally the last school bell of the day rang.

The children squealed with delight as they all jumped to their feet, slinging their backpacks over their shoulders.

"Hold on just a minute!" she shouted above the noise of their scuffling feet as they raced toward the door.

THE HIGH COUNTRY

"Don't forget our field trip next week. I need those permission slips signed and returned to me on Monday," she said to the backs of their heads as they headed toward the door. "No permission slip, no trip. Got it?"

The class shouted a response in unison, "Got it!"

She followed her class down the hall and walked them to their respective bus line assuring that each one was on the correct bus before heading back to her classroom.

Once there she collected her things, turned off the lights and locked the door.

She let out a sigh of relief as she reached her car and opened the door. She decided to stop at the Safeway that was closest to her home.

Inside the grocery store, she picked up the items for a salad, two thick steaks, a couple of large baking potatoes, the ingredients for the cake and a bottle of Cabernet Sauvignon.

Satisfied with her selections she went to the register and paid for the items. As she headed back to the car, she could already feel the stresses of the week fading away.

She was already thinking about the time she would be spending with Trevor. She was smiling so big that you probably could have seen it from the moon, but that was okay with her.

The thought of spending any amount of time with that gorgeous man would make any woman smile.

Molly finished spreading the hot coals around in the small kettle grill and replaced the cooking grate. She stepped back through her double French doors to get the steaks as her front doorbell rang.

She found Trevor standing on the other side of the door with a bottle of wine in one hand and a bouquet of flowers in the other.

"Hope I'm not too early," he said handing her the flowers. "These are for you. Emily told me I had better not show up without them."

"Well, I thank both of you. They're lovely," she said as she headed to the kitchen for a vase. "I need to put these in some water before they wilt. Make yourself comfortable."

Instead, he followed her into the kitchen.

"Where should I put this?" he asked, still holding the wine.

Molly went to a drawer and got out a corkscrew and handed it to him.

"Can you open it and pour us a glass? The glasses are in that cabinet there," she said pointing to it with a pair of tongs.

"I was just about to put the steaks on," she continued as she picked up the plate with the marinating steaks on it and headed back outside to put them on the grill.

A few minutes later, she returned and Trevor handed her a glass of the wine.

"Thank you, sir," she said as she took the glass and swirled the dark liquid. She brought the glass to her nose and sniffed its contents.

"Nice bouquet," she said. Taking a small sip, she continued, "Refreshing taste. Nice choice."

"You have to thank Emily for that too I'm afraid," he admitted. "The bottle was sitting on the kitchen table when I got home. I'm more of a beer man myself, but I can adapt."

"Well, here's to adaptation," she said as she raised her glass to him.

He returned the gesture and they clinked the glasses together.

"To adaptation," he concurred as he took his first sip.

He had tried to keep telling himself that this wasn't a date, but who was he trying to kid? It looked like it might turn out to be just that.

And that might not be such a bad thing.

THE HIGH COUNTRY

Caroline was standing on her tip-toes on the middle rail of the corral holding out a long carrot.

"Chocolate, come here girl," she said as she wiggled the carrot back and forth. "Come and get it."

The horse raised her head and snorted, bobbing her head up and down, making her mane sway with the motion. Slowly the horse started walking in the young girl's direction.

"That's it, come on," she coaxed still waving the carrot. "You know it's your favorite."

Chocolate had just taken the carrot when the back door opened and Emily called to her.

"Your dinner is ready young lady. You had better come in and eat it before it gets cold," she said.

"I'm coming," Caroline replied as she patted her horse on the neck. "I'll try to come back later girl."

The horse snorted and nodded again as if she understood and was acknowledging her.

Caroline jumped down from the railing and ran toward the house.

Emily was putting the last bowl on the table as the child came through the door and went to take her place at the table.

"Uh, uh, uh," Emily admonished. "You know better than that. You know you have to wash your hands after you feed or touch that horse missy."

"Yes ma'am," said Caroline as she turned and went to the kitchen sink and ran the water.

After rinsing the suds off her hands, Caroline wiped them on a dishtowel and returned to her spot at the table.

"Much better," Emily said as she picked up Caroline's plate and filled it with the girl's favorite foods. Emily had prepared the meal knowing that Trevor wouldn't be home and knowing that Caroline wouldn't be happy about his dinner plans.

Eli was nestled in his high chair to the right of Emily's chair. He was jabbering happily. She went to the pantry and got a jar of sweet potatoes which Eli loved. He slapped the tray of the chair impatiently.

"You hold your horses young man," Emily scolded. Eli just slapped the tray again and gurgled loudly. He started bobbing up and down in his seat when he heard the distinctive pop from the seal of the lid of the jar. His mouth was already open awaiting his first bite even before Emily could even take her seat.

Caroline looked at the table settings and got a puzzled look on her face.

"Why are there only two plates? Where's Daddy? Isn't he going to eat with us?" Caroline asked.

"He had other plans for dinner tonight, but you need to eat yours before it gets cold. After dinner, I'm going to give your brother his bath and then it's your turn," Emily answered.

"Okay," Caroline responded. "Will Daddy be home in time to read me my bedtime story?"

"I'm afraid I can't answer that. He didn't tell me what time to expect him. If he's not back, I'll read you one. Will that be okay?" replied Emily.

"I guess so, but can I give Chocolate another carrot while Eli has his bath?" Caroline asked.

"As long as it's just one. You don't want to spoil her now, do you?" Emily said.

"Just one, I promise," replied Caroline as she scooped a fork full of her macaroni and cheese and brought it to her mouth.

After Caroline finished her meal, she got up and put her dirty plate into the sink.

She ran over to the refrigerator and grabbed the treat for her horse. Carrot in hand, she practically raced to the corral.

THE HIGH COUNTRY

Jumping back up on the railing she held out the treat for the horse, but this time Chocolate didn't take much coaxing.

She gently took the offered carrot from Caroline's hand, munching happily.

"I forgot to ask you, how do you like your steak cooked?" Molly asked.

"Is there any way to cook a steak other than medium rare?" Trevor asked.

"Not for me there isn't. I'm glad you like them cooked that way as well," Molly responded as she sat down at the patio table.

"Oh, I almost forgot. I sent a permission slip for a field trip home with the children yesterday. I need the slips signed and returned to me by Monday, but I'm sure that Caroline must have told you about it already," Molly said as she sipped the last of her wine. She set the empty glass on the glass table top.

"No, she didn't mention it. It probably slipped her mind. She has been very distracted lately," Trevor replied as he joined her at the table.

"Where are you taking them?" he asked, taking a sip of the wine himself.

"Just to a ranch in over in Laramie," she replied. "They have some baby goats, lambs and calves right now. It's kind of like a petting zoo. I thought the kids would like to visit a working cattle and horse ranch."

"It's not gonna be anything new for Caroline. After all, she *lives* on a working ranch," he countered.

"I know, but the others don't," she said as she stood.

"I'd better check the steaks. Can you check on the potatoes for me?" she asked as she stood and walked over to the kettle grill and removed the lid.

"Sure thing," he replied as he picked up her glass and headed back inside.

"Looks like you need a refill," he said.

She didn't even have a chance to protest. *He definitely has potential*, she thought.

CHAPTER FOURTEEN

CAROLINE STEPPED OUT of the tub and Emily wrapped a soft terry cloth towel around her small frame.

"I guess I'm gonna be reading you your bedtime story tonight. You go get your PJ's on and pick one out. I'm going to check in on Eli really quick and be right there," Emily promised.

"Okay," replied Caroline as she pulled the towel tight around herself and scurried off to her room.

Emily walked softly down the hallway to the nursery and peeked inside. By the glow of his nightlight, Emily could see that he was sleeping soundly. She tip-toed in and replaced the blanket that he had kicked off while he was fighting sleep. He stirred briefly but settled back into slumber just as quickly.

Emily found Caroline sitting up in bed, under the covers with an Aesop's Fables book in her lap. She was leafing through the pages until she found the story she wanted.

"This one," she decided as she handed Emily the book.

"Oh, that's a good one," Emily said as she took the book and started reading aloud. "There once was this lion…."

Molly stepped back into the kitchen as Trevor was putting the cork back into the wine bottle. He looked up and held her glass out to her.

She smiled, took it and took a small sip. Tilting her head just slightly she looked at him with a pondering expression.

"*What?*" asked Trevor, suspiciously.

"I was just wondering if you would mind telling me what happened to Caroline's mother. If it's too painful, I understand. It's just that I thought it might help me to better understand what is going on with her," Molly said.

"It's okay," Trevor said. "Her name was Beth. Right after our son Eli was born, Beth was diagnosed with ovarian cancer. The doctors did everything that they could, but it wasn't enough. She passed away when our son was only nine months old."

"Caroline and Beth were very close. Caroline was there and saw everything that was happening to her mother. I think it made her mad at all the doctors who couldn't make Beth better. Maybe even mad at the world in general," he continued.

"That does explain a lot of things that I have seen from her. No wonder she's lashing out at everyone and everything. Do you want me to see if I can get her in to see the school guidance counselor?" she asked.

"That might not be a bad idea, thanks," he admitted.

"I'll talk to her first thing Monday morning," she promised.

THE HIGH COUNTRY

As Emily finished the story, she looked over at Caroline. Her head was nestled against her hand and she looked like a sleeping angel.

Emily gently closed the story book and placed it on the bedside table. She rose and walked to the door, flipping off the light as she left the room.

"Sleep well, little one," she whispered to the sleeping child.

Caroline stirred, but didn't wake. She walked down the hall to check on Eli.

After they finished their meal, Molly and Trevor gathered the dirty dishes and put them in the sink. Molly rinsed the plates before putting them in the dishwasher.

"I'll start this thing later tonight," she said. "I don't want to fool with it right now."

"I don't really blame you," Trevor replied. "I'm glad that I have Emily for that sort of thing. She helps me with the kids too. She's great."

"Emily is..." Molly questioned, feeling a little jealous.

"Oh, sorry," Trevor replied. "Emily is our housekeeper and nanny. You've met her, but I forgot that you were never properly introduced that night. I had other things on my mind."

Like me, she thought.

Trevor turned toward Molly and cupped her face with both hands. He looked deeply into her emerald green eyes.

"I am so glad that you didn't get hurt that day," he admitted.

He leaned toward Molly and placed his lips on hers and kissed her tenderly. Molly immediately responded to his kiss, feeling a warm and tingling sensation run though her entire body. It felt like it went to her very soul.

Trevor parted her lips with his tongue and began exploring her mouth. Twirling his tongue around hers, tickling the roof of her mouth. Molly tilted her head and wrapped her arms around his neck, pulling him closer and returning the kiss just as passionately.

Trevor abruptly ended the kiss and looked her in the eyes again. Molly was still reeling from the experience.

"I've been wanting to do that for a while now," he whispered in a sultry voice.

"And I'm so glad that you did," Molly admitted, still feeling a little flushed.

Trevor touched his lips to hers again, tenderly. Pulling her close to his chest he tenderly kissed the curve of her neck, inhaling a familiar scent coming from her hair. He ran his fingers through her locks pulling them closer to his face.

"Oh, Beth," he whispered softly against her neck.

Molly tensed and put her hand against his chest and gently pushed away from his embrace.

"What did you just say?" she asked, feeling agitated.

Trevor reached to pull her back into the embrace, but Molly resisted, her hand still resting on Trevor's chest.

"What's wrong?" he asked, completely unaware of what he had just done.

"What's wrong?" she repeated, incredulously. She walked away from him and started wiping the counter near the stove, fighting back the tears that were welling up in her eyes.

Trevor came up behind her and touched her arm. She pulled it away and turned to face him.

"I think it's best if you were to leave now," was all she said, her lip quivering. A single tear ran down her cheek.

"Are you going to answer my question?" he asked.

"Please, just go," was her response.

"But…" he started to reply.

"But nothing. Just please, go now," she said.

THE HIGH COUNTRY

Puzzled, Trevor picked up his hat from the post on the back of the chair and walked, dejectedly, toward the door. Stopping before he reached it, he turned.

"Can I at least call you later?" he asked.

Molly didn't answer him, but instead returned to her cleaning task.

Trevor shrugged, put his hat on his head and walked out the door.

What the hell did I do? he thought. He started his truck, threw his hat on the seat and pulled out of the driveway.

The drive back to High Country was less than pleasant for Trevor as he racked his brain trying to determine the cause of Molly's sudden mood shift tonight.

The radio in his truck was playing a twangy country music song. He reached forward and switched it off. He wanted to remember the events of the night and needed to concentrate.

Going over the conversation in his head, he couldn't remember anything that could have warranted such a response from Molly.

The kiss had been wonderful. He thought of the smell of her hair as he'd nuzzled her neck. That familiar scent. Beth had used the same shampoo. He'd loved the smell of her hair just after she had washed it.

Then it hit him.

Oh, shit, please tell me I didn't, he thought. *Fuck, I think I did. I called her Beth.*

No wonder she got upset with me, I'm such a fucking idiot.

He slammed his palms against the steering wheel, then ran the index finger of his right hand across his mouth.

Why do I always let you get me in trouble, he thought, still rubbing the offending culprit.

Molly threw the dish rag onto the counter as soon as the door closed behind Trevor. She let the tears welling in her eyes freely cascade down her cheeks. She wiped her cheek with the back of her hand and returned to loading the dishwasher.

What were you expecting Molly? She thought.

One thing she knew for certain. She was definitely falling for this man, but how do you compete with a ghost?

I want him to love me for who I am, I don't want to be a surrogate for his late wife.

She loaded the last of the dishes into the machine and put a detergent tablet into the dispensing tray. Closing the door, she set the timer for a four-hour delay wash cycle. That way it would run tonight while she slept.

After pouring herself another glass of wine, she went into her bathroom and started the tap running in the bathtub.

She wanted a nice, long, hot bath. One that was, as her grandfather used to say, '*Hot enough to boil your hams*'.

She wanted to relax, sip her wine, soak until her fingertips looked like prunes and the water turned cold.

I need time to think, she thought.

CHAPTER FIFTEEN

TREVOR SAW THE lights were still on in the kitchen as he pulled his truck into its usual spot beside the barn.

Great, he thought sarcastically, *Emily is still up.*

Dreading the conversation that he knew was coming, he walked through the mudroom door and into the kitchen.

Emily was sitting at the breakfast nook table drinking a cup of hot chocolate and reading the Cheyenne Gazette. She looked up as he approached.

"*Well?*" she asked as he removed his hat and hung it from the rack beside the door.

"Do you have a shoe horn big enough to get this size eleven boot out of my mouth?" he responded lifting his right foot.

"Went that well, huh?" she said as she laid the newspaper on the table. Patting the chair beside her she said, "Come here, tell me what happened."

He sat down in the offered chair, sighing heavily, but didn't say anything.

Leaning back, he ran his fingers through his short, wavy brown hair.

"It can't be as bad as you're letting on," she continued.

"I'd just as soon forget the whole thing," Trevor said finally. "Are the kids okay? Did they give you any trouble?"

"Both of them were little angels, but don't you think for one minute that you're getting off that easy," she chided. "Spill already."

"Well, if you must know, it was going great. Right up until I whispered Beth's name into her ear," he admitted.

"Oh, I see," Emily replied.

"I didn't realize I'd done it until I was halfway home. All I knew at the time was that she suddenly got really upset with me and asked me to leave."

"That's not *too* terribly bad," she said soothingly.

"Bad enough for her to kick me out," he said. "I asked if I could call her later, but she ignored me. To tell you the truth, I don't blame *her* for being upset, I blame me."

"All you gotta do is give her some time. Time to cool off and to think. When you call her, invite her out for coffee or something. Try to explain things and smooth it over as best you can," Emily said.

"You make it sound so simple," he said.

"I wish it was," Emily admitted. "But if you explain yourself right, I'm sure that she'll understand and find it in her heart to forgive you."

"Can you help me with that?" he asked.

"Afraid not," she said. "It's gotta come from you, but you have a little time to think of what you want to say. You'll be fine, you'll see. Just give her about a week."

She patted the back of his hand as she stood, picked up the paper, folded it and put it under arm. She put her mug in the sink and turned out the light above the window.

"I'm tired, sir," she said as she turned and faced Trevor. Leaning against the sink, she said, "If you don't mind, I'm gonna call it a night."

"Goodnight Emily, and thanks."

THE HIGH COUNTRY

"For what?" Emily said as she winked and started to leave the room. "I have no idea what you're talking about."

Trevor smiled and shook his head.

Why are some women so complicated? He thought, *and others so wise.*

Trevor got up the next morning before sunrise, had Maverick saddled and was halfway to the northwest fence line as the sun crested over the ridge.

He had already called Logan and they had agreed to finish checking the remaining fencing. Logan was riding the south end of the fence line, Trevor the north. They would meet in the middle and discuss their findings.

Trevor had just finished checking his section and wasn't surprised to see Logan coming over the hill.

"Whatcha find?" Trevor asked.

"Not as bad as we thought," Logan replied. "Only two posts on the southwest side. We should have enough material for that. You?"

"Six posts and a section of wire. We should be good then. We have enough material for all of it," Trevor said.

"Well, let's get to it then," Trevor gently nudged Maverick's sides to get him moving again.

"Right behind ya," replied Logan as he, too, nudged his horse into motion.

"You gonna tell me how your date went?" asked Logan.

"Nope," was all Trevor said.

Molly stepped out of the shower and wrapped a terry cloth towel around her head. She grabbed the other towel from the rack on the wall and wrapped that one around her slender frame.

Walking over to her closet, she selected a blue sweater and a pair of grey slacks. She lay them across the bed and went back to the bathroom. Removing the towel, she rubbed it over her locks to remove a little more of the moisture.

Picking up a comb, she ran it through her hair and removed a mass of tangles. Picking up the hair dryer, she turned it on and started drying her hair.

She had left her cell phone on the dresser. The screen lit up as it started ringing.

Molly couldn't hear it over the noise of the hair dryer. After a few rings the screen became dark again.

Molly hadn't noticed. She got ready and left for work, scooping up her cell phone on the way to her car.

Looking at the clock on the wall in the living room, she realized that she was going to be cutting it close. She just hoped she could get to the school in time.

I'll have to speed, she thought, *but just a little.*

Trevor left the voicemail and put his cell phone back in his pocket. He was hoping to catch Molly before she left for work.

I know Emily told me to wait a week, he thought, *but I can't let it go on that long.*

Smiling he turned around in his saddle and saw that Logan was gaining on him. Trevor pulled slightly on Maverick's reins to slow his pace, but not by much.

"Everything okay?" Logan asked as pulled his horse alongside Maverick.

"Yeah," replied Trevor. "I was just following up on something at the feed store."

Logan chuckled and gave Trevor a 'yeah right' look.

THE HIGH COUNTRY

"The damaged section is right over this crest," Logan said pointing to the ridgeline.

"We'll have to bring more supplies up after lunch," Trevor said. "Since there are only two posts on the southwest side, we'll do those first. We have the posts up here, right?"

"For that section, yeah. But we'll need to use the truck after lunch though," replied Logan. "We've used almost all of the posts we brought up last trip."

They topped the hill and Trevor immediately saw what Logan was talking about.

Both men pulled the reins, brought their horses to a stop and dismounted. They tied the horses to an undamaged section of the fencing, picked up the post hole diggers and got to work.

Molly arrived at the elementary school as the busses were still unloading. She entered the building and hurried down the hallway to her classroom.

She threw her purse on her desk as the first of her students started to trickle in. When the purse landed on the desk her cellphone fell out, which forced the screen to light up.

It was then that she saw the missed call and voicemail message on the screen. She smiled when she saw that the call was Trevor.

I'll have to listen to the message later, she thought. *I don't have time right now.*

As the last of her students took their seats she said, "Are you ready for your spelling test today?"

That question was met with groans from the entire classroom.

"Oh, it's not that bad. Right now, though, I want you to get out your science books and turn to page thirty-two," Molly instructed.

There was a shuffling of chairs and backpacks as the students worked to comply with her instructions.

"Can anyone tell me what a baby frog is called?" she asked.

Several hands went up immediately, and she picked a thin, pale boy in the back row.

"Yes, Derek," she said, pointing to the child.

"Toad?" he said sheepishly.

The other students giggled and Derek blushed, looking slightly embarrassed.

"Now, we'll have none of that," Molly admonished the classroom.

"No, Derek, it's not a toad, but you're close. It's called a tadpole. They are also amphibians."

Molly went to the dry erase board and wrote the big word on it.

"That means that they can live in and out of the water," she said. "There are very few animals that can do this."

Another boy in the second row raised his hand.

Molly looked at him and said, "Yes, Hunter?"

"My grandpa calls me tadpole. Does that mean that I'm an an-pib-be-yan?" he asked, struggling with the word.

The class giggled again, and Molly gave them a stern look.

"No honey. That's just your grandpa's nickname for you."

"Good," replied Hunter. "'Cause I can't swim."

"That's a good thing to know. Now, can anyone tell me something else about frogs?" Molly asked.

Little hands shot up around the room. Every student had their hand raised except for one, Caroline.

THE HIGH COUNTRY

She was staring blankly out the window. Caroline had a bad habit of doing that. Molly made a mental note to speak to Trevor about it when she returned his call.

Molly had just collected the spelling test when the lunch bell rang. There was a scuffling of desk chairs as the children rose from their seats.

"Just a minute," Molly said. "Hunter is the leader for today. I need you to line up, single file, behind him please."

The children did as she instructed as she escorted her class to the cafeteria. Once they were safely inside she went to the teacher's lounge to heat her lunch.

She sat down in one of the arm chairs in the corner of the room, pulled her cellphone from her pocket and touched several icons to pull up the voicemail screen. She pushed the play button and put the phone to her ear. This is what she heard:

"Hi Molly, it's me. I have felt like such an idiot since Saturday night. I didn't even realize what I had done until I was halfway home. Can you forgive me? How can I make it up to you? Please call me. I need to talk to you about a few things. You have my number, Bye."

Molly touched the call back button to return the call. Trevor answered on the second ring.

"Hello," he said.

"Hey," she said. "I only have a few minutes, so I'll make this quick. We do have a lot to discuss and I am going to give you a do-over, but just one. My place Saturday night at 7:00 o'clock. Don't be late."

"Yes, ma'am," replied Trevor eagerly.

"Good," replied Molly. "I'll see you then and by the way, I love roses."

"I look forward to it and thanks for the head's up. I'll talk to you later then, bye," he said.

"Bye," she replied. The phone beeped twice, and the screen went dark.

There may be hope for him yet, she thought.

Trevor was smiling broadly as he put his phone back in his pocket. Logan couldn't help but notice. He put the blades of the post hole diggers on the ground and leaned on the handles.

"Well don't you look like the cat that just ate the canary?" he said teasingly.

"What are you talking about?" replied Trevor.

"And answering a question with a question," answered Logan. "You know good and well what I'm talking about."

"That was Caroline's teacher. She has a few things she wants to discuss with me, that's all," Trevor said.

"I'll bet she does," Logan said, mockingly.

"Will you knock it off. I'm not paying you to stand here and harass me about my personal phone calls. We have work to do," Trevor admonished.

There is something going on there, Logan thought. *I think I just hit a nerve.*

CHAPTER SIXTEEN

MOLLY WOKE EARLIER than she usually did on most other Saturdays. She was excited about the idea of spending more time with Trevor tonight.

With so much to do in preparation for the evening, she made a to-do list and put it on the counter. She also made a grocery list for later. She planned on making Italian tonight. Linguini with clam sauce, Caesar salad and garlic bread.

She also had a nice bottle of wine chilling in the fridge. She got a vase from under the sink just in case Trevor had gotten her hint.

She picked up her keys and headed to her car. Best to get the shopping out of the way first. She was out of Windex and Fantastik and she needed both for cleaning the bathroom.

Emily walked into the kitchen and found Trevor standing at the sink, drinking a cup of coffee and looking out the window.

"Well, you're up early, as usual," she said.

"Yeah, I thought about taking Caroline on a short trail ride this morning. I haven't been spending much time with her lately. Thought she might like that," Trevor said.

"*Like it.* She'd absolutely love it," Emily replied.

"Is she up yet?" he asked.

"Not yet," Emily replied. "I was going to let her sleep until breakfast was ready, but now I have a better idea. Why don't I fix your breakfast to go? That way she can eat on the trail with you like a real cow-hand."

"That sounds like a great idea. I'll go saddle the horses while you get breakfast ready. Then, I'll go wake her. She'll be so excited."

"We'll probably be back before lunch," Trevor continued. "Oh, by the way, I have dinner plans tonight."

"Again?" Emily asked as she raised her eyebrow.

"I just couldn't leave it like that," he admitted.

"You can fill me in on the details later," Emily said. "Right now, you tend to the horses. I'll tend to breakfast."

"Deal," he said as he headed out the back door.

No sooner than the door had closed, Caroline bounded into the kitchen full of energy.

"I thought I heard Daddy," she said.

"You did," Emily replied. "You just missed him. He went out to the barn."

Caroline ran to the refrigerator and grabbed a couple of carrots for her horse. Before Emily could stop her, she was already out the door.

Running across the gravel drive, she twisted her ankle on the loose stones. She went down in a heap, scraping her right knee in the process.

She issued a short squeal as she turned and clutched the injured leg.

Trevor heard her and came running out of the barn. Seeing his daughter on the dirt and clutching her leg he ran to her.

THE HIGH COUNTRY

"What happened?" he asked as he knelt beside the small child.

"I was in a hurry to get these carrots to Chocolate and I fell," she said. "My knee hurts."

Trevor scooped up his daughter and headed back to the kitchen. Caroline was still clutching the carrots.

"What about these?" Caroline asked, holding up the carrots.

"Those can wait," said her father. "We need to get you cleaned up and bandaged. You can't go on a trail ride without a bandage on a scrape like that."

Caroline beamed at that thought.

"Really Daddy? A real trail ride?" she asked.

"Yep," he replied. "I was putting the saddle on Chocolate when I heard you cry out."

Trevor walked into the kitchen as Emily was putting their breakfast into paper bags. He went to the table and put Caroline into one of the chairs.

"What happened?" Emily asked.

"I fell," was all that Caroline said.

"Well, let me have a look," Emily said. "It doesn't look too bad. Just some antiseptic, Neosporin and a Band-Aid and you'll be good as new."

"Goodie!" exclaimed Caroline. "I wanna go on the trail ride with Daddy."

"I thought it was supposed to be a surprise," Emily said as she went to the cabinet containing the first-aid kit.

"It was," he responded. "That is, until *she* surprised *me*."

Kneeling in front of Caroline, Emily cleaned the wound, applied the ointment to a Band-Aid, covered the scrape with it and assured the child that she was going to live.

Delighted with the prognosis, Caroline jumped up from the chair and ran to the back door.

"Whoa!" said Trevor. "Where are you headed?"

"You said these could wait," replied Caroline, holding up the carrots again. "But Chocolate is hungry."

"Well then, I guess we can't keep her waiting," replied Trevor. "Go on out. I'll be back out in a minute."

"Here you go sir," said Emily as she handed Trevor the two brown paper bags containing their breakfast.

"I'll have your lunch ready for you when you return," she continued.

"Thanks, Emily," said Trevor. "I really don't know what I'd do without you."

Trevor headed out the back door to join Caroline at the barn. The child, as expected, was standing on the rail to Chocolate's stall. Her small hand was stroking the neck of the horse.

"Ready to go?" Trevor asked.

"Yeah!" shouted the small child.

Since Caroline's legs were not long enough to reach the stirrups on her own, Trevor hoisted the child up into the saddle and handed her the reins.

"You think you can do it on your own this time?" Trevor asked.

"Of course, Daddy," she replied. "Can't you see that I'm a big girl now."

"I see that," he conceded. "Well, I guess we can go now."

He tapped his heels on Maverick's sides to get the horse in motion. Trevor knew that Chocolate would instinctively follow Maverick, so he wasn't too concerned with Caroline's equestrian abilities.

They were headed to Beth's favorite picnic spot. A small meadow on the top of the ridge that was a mile and a half in front of them.

He hadn't been to this spot since he had taken Beth, right after her initial diagnosis. It was going to be tough for him, but he was doing this for Caroline.

Thirty minutes later the clearing came into view and Trevor led Maverick to a nice, shady spot and dismounted. He tied the horse's reins to a small sapling. He lifted Caroline

THE HIGH COUNTRY

from her saddle and helped her to the ground. He reached into her saddle bag and removed a picnic blanket that he had stowed there earlier.

With a flick of his wrists he laid the blanket on a grassy spot under one of the large oak trees that bordered the clearing.

"This is perfect," said Caroline as Trevor tied Chocolate to another sapling nearby.

"I thought you'd like it," Trevor replied.

"What did Emily make us for breakfast?" Caroline asked.

"Well, let's see," replied Trevor as he removed the paper bags from his saddle bags and handed one to her.

Inside the bag was a carton of milk, a bacon and cheese biscuit and an apple.

As soon as Trevor saw the apple he knew that Caroline wouldn't be the one eating it, and he was right.

No sooner than Caroline finished her biscuit and milk, she headed to Chocolate with the apple.

"You're spoiling her," Trevor scolded.

"She's hungry too," countered Caroline.

"Alright, but she's not getting mine," said Trevor as he took a big bite of his apple.

Caroline held the fruit up to horse and Chocolate nibbled at it but knocked it out of the girl's hand. Caroline picked it up and brushed off the dirt and leaves that clung to it.

Chocolate finished her apple and Caroline joined Trevor on the picnic blanket. She had only been sitting there for a few minutes when a yellow and black butterfly landed on her hairbow on the top of her head.

Trevor chuckled and said, "Hold really still."

Caroline's eyes were framed with panic, but she remained still.

"What's wrong Daddy?" she asked, still showing a look of panic.

"Nothing, baby," he soothed. "A butterfly is sitting on your head. I want to get a picture of it to show Emily."

"Really?" she asked skeptically.

"I'm not kidding," he replied. "It's on your hairbow." He slowly pulled out his cellphone and opened the camera app. Holding the phone out toward Caroline, he pushed the shutter release button. Upon the click of the shutter, the butterfly flew away and Caroline saw it for the first time.

"You weren't kidding," she said as she watched it flutter away. "Can I see the picture?"

"Sure," said Trevor as he held out the phone for his daughter to see. "But we're gonna have to be headed back soon."

"Already?" asked Caroline with a hint of disappointment.

"Afraid so," replied Trevor. "But we'll stay just a little while longer if you like."

"Yes, please," replied Caroline.

CHAPTER SEVENTEEN

TREVOR WAS STANDING on Molly's front porch at exactly 6:55 p.m. He stood there for several minutes nervously shifting his weight from one foot to the other. When he reached out to ring the doorbell he was startled when the door suddenly opened to reveal Molly on the other side.

"Well, are you coming in or are you going to stand *there* all night?" she asked.

"I was getting there, but you beat me to it," he replied as he crossed the threshold and entered the room.

"Make yourself comfortable," she said as she headed to the kitchen. "I just need to check on our dinner and I'll be right back. Would you like a beer? Or possibly a glass of wine?"

"I'll take a beer please," he replied. "What kind do you have?"

Molly went to the fridge, opened it and replied, "I have Corona, but no limes. I have Michelob Ultra and Coors light."

"The Ultra please," he replied.

"You got it."

She opened the freezer drawer and removed a glass from a pull-out tray. Opening the beer, she tilted the glass slightly before starting to pour the brew into the frosty glass. This prevented the beer from getting too much of a head on it.

Handing the beer to Trevor she said, "Here ya go."

"Wow, even in a cold glass," he responded as he took the offered drink. "You're gonna spoil me."

"That's my intention," she replied, smiling wryly.

Trevor lifted one eyebrow at her remark but said nothing. Instead he took a sip of the beer, swallowed it and let out a sigh.

"Is something wrong?" Molly asked.

"No, everything is great," he replied.

"Good," said Molly as she turned to return to the kitchen. Trevor stood and followed her.

"Is there anything I can do to help you?" he asked.

"Other than keeping me company, not really," she replied.

Trevor pulled out one of the stools that lined the bar countertop and sat down and watched her stir a pot on the stove.

Her back was turned to him and he couldn't help but stare at her backside. *How have I not noticed that gorgeous rump before*, he thought.

He cleared his throat and looked down at his drink, hoping she hadn't noticed. She seemed oblivious as she lifted the spoon to her lips and tasted the sauce. Not satisfied with the flavor, she picked up the rosemary and sprinkled a little into the sauce and stirred.

"It'll be ready in about ten minutes," she said as she opened the fridge again. This time she removed a bottle of wine and sat it on the counter.

Opening the cabinet above her head she took out a wine glass and shut the door. She poured herself a glass and joined Trevor at the bar.

THE HIGH COUNTRY

"I'm going to let the sauce simmer for a while before I start the noodles. Hope you like Italian." she said.

"Smells wonderful," he answered. "What is it?"

"Linguini with clam sauce. There are Caesar salads in the fridge and garlic bread in the oven."

"You didn't have to go to so much trouble," he said.

"It's no trouble. I love to cook," she answered. "Speaking of which, I'd better get the linguini going now."

She stood and went back to the counter. Opening the cabinet below the counter she removed a large metal pot.

Taking it over to the sink, she filled it with water. Placing it on the grate covering the element on the stove, she turned on the burner.

"Better make that fifteen minutes," she said as she picked up her glass and took a sip of her wine.

Trevor looked her up and down appraisingly. "I'm in no hurry," he admitted.

Molly looked at him and smiled.

Emily dodged as a splash of water narrowly missed her. It was coming from the bathtub.

It was the children's bath time and to save time tonight, she had decided to try and bathe them together. However, she didn't think that she would wind up getting a bath too.

Eli was slapping his hands on the top of the water and taking great delight in the sound it made. He laughed each time Emily dodged his splashing. Caroline was drawing on the back of the tub wall with her soap crayons. Tonight, she told Emily that she was trying to draw a mermaid. To Emily it resembled a trout more than a mermaid, but she didn't tell Caroline that.

After a few minutes, Caroline turned to look at Emily and asked, "Is Daddy going to be home in time to read me my bedtime story tonight?"

"I don't think so dear," replied Emily. "I will read one to both of you at the same time. How's that?"

"I guess it'll be okay," conceded Caroline. The child looked at her fingers and got a puzzled look on her face.

"Something wrong?" asked Emily.

"My fingers are all wrinkly," complained Caroline.

"Well, that means it's time to get out of the tub," said Emily. She helped Caroline over the tub wall and wrapped a towel around her small frame.

"What about my hair?" asked Caroline. "It's still wet."

Emily grabbed a towel from under the vanity and wrapped it around Caroline's curly but dripping hair.

"You go on to your room and pick out your pajamas while I get your brother ready for bed. I'll be in to comb and dry your hair after I put him in his crib."

"What about the story?" Caroline reminded.

"After we dry your hair, we'll sit in the rocking chair in the nursery. The one beside the crib. I'll let you sit in my lap while I read. That way Eli can hear it too.

"Okay," Caroline said. "I'll get his favorite book then. The one where you have to make all of the animal noises. He likes that."

"Fine," replied Emily. "It won't take me but a minute to get him ready. You go ahead and get yourself ready for bed, okay."

"Okay," Caroline answered as she trotted loudly down the hallway to her room

Emily picked up the squirming baby from the tub and put him on the towel that she had draped over her lap. Eli looked up at her, gurgling happily. She wrapped him in the warm terry cloth and took him to the nursery.

THE HIGH COUNTRY

It took almost five minutes to get his diaper on because he kept wriggling away from her. Once she had succeeded with that task, his pajamas were easy.

She kissed the top of his head and put him down in the crib.

Then she went to assist Caroline with her night-time routine. Sometimes she needed to be reminded to brush her teeth.

Trevor picked up his napkin and wiped his mouth and chin. Throwing the napkin into his plate he said, "That was delicious." Molly smiled at him across her patio table.

"Thank you, sir," Molly said as she too placed her napkin on her plate.

Trevor stood, took both of their plates and headed inside, to the kitchen. He walked over to the sink, turned on the tap, and started rinsing the dishes.

"You don't have to do that," Molly said. "I was going to run the dishwasher later tonight."

"Not a problem," Trevor replied. "Just knocking off the big chunks." After he rinsed the plates and put them into the machine, then he looked around the kitchen. He spotted a bowl and several spoons. He gave them a quick rinse before putting them into the dishwasher as well.

"There," he said as he wiped his hands on a dish towel. "That didn't take me long and it wasn't any trouble."

Molly watched as Trevor completed his task and turned to face her. He leaned back on the sink and she couldn't help but notice the ripples of his abs under the thin fabric of his shirt. It was unbuttoned to mid-chest and it gave her a glimpse of his pectoral muscles as well.

"Hmmm…" said Molly softly.

"What was that?" asked Trevor, having barely heard her.

"Nothing," Molly said, blushing. "I was just thinking."

"About what?" he asked.

"This," she said as she stepped closer to him. Grabbing the front of his shirt she pulled him close, placing her lips softly on his and kissed him tenderly. Trevor responded by opening his lips and tenderly exploring her mouth with his tongue.

As her tongue entwined with his, a shiver ran down her spine. It ignited a spark and fueled a passion inside her that had not existed in her for a very long time.

Her right hand caressed the front of his shirt, feeling the ripples of his gorgeous chest. Her hand slipped beneath the thin fabric of his shirt and she let it wander across his chest to his nipple. She brushed it, ever so tenderly with her fingers, and felt it become firm to her touch.

Molly turned her head, breaking the kiss and rested her forehead against the curve of his neck. She left her hand where it was.

"Well, that was something I have been thinking about too," he admitted as he put his index finger under her chin and tilted her head so that she was facing him once more.

"A lot," he continued. He pushed a hand into her hair at the nape of her neck and kissed her deeply, passionately. Molly responded in kind opening her mouth to his probing tongue.

Trevor let his other hand move to her breast and cupped it tenderly.

Molly placed her hand over his and pulled away from his kiss.

"Is something wrong?" he asked.

"No," she responded. "I just thought we'd be more comfortable if we went to my room."

She took his hand that was clutching her breast to lead him down the hallway.

They had hardly gone two steps when he pulled her hand toward him causing her to turn and face him.

THE HIGH COUNTRY

"What…" Molly started, but she was cut short by his mouth covering hers in a tender kiss. Before the kiss ended, Trevor scooped her up in his arms to carry her the rest of the way down the hall.

Molly put her hand on his chest and again pulled back from the kiss.

"There is only one problem with this," she said.

Trevor stopped walking and looked down at her with a concerned expression.

"Oh, what's that?" he asked cautiously.

"You don't know which one of these rooms is mine," she responded pointing to the closed doors that lined the hallway.

"And?" he asked.

"Second one on the right," she answered.

"There," he said. "Problem solved." He continued to the door she indicated, turning the knob with the hand that was nestled under the crook of her knees.

He pushed the door open with his boot and stepped inside, not taking the time to push it shut.

He hurried over to the side of the bed and eased her gently down in the middle. He joined her as he was lowering her.

As soon as her back touched the bed he buried his face against the side of her neck, lightly kissing the soft curve just below her left ear.

The touch of his tongue against her skin sent a tingle down her spine but it didn't end there. The tingle managed to make it all the way to her clit. She shivered with the wonderful sensation.

Trevor took this as a sign of encouragement and took her earlobe into his mouth, sucking gently. His breath against her ear, sent a series of tingles following the first. She snuggled closer to him, wanting more.

Trevor obliged. His hand went to the buttons of her blouse and he started to unbutton it, slowly and methodically.

Once the blouse was completely unbuttoned, he slipped his hand underneath her. He was searching for the clasp of her bra. He found it and released her breasts from the material with a flick of his fingers.

He started kissing her skin, starting from the nape of her neck, but he had every intention of working his way down to the soft mounds that were still covered by her bra.

When he got to her shoulders he pushed the blouse down her arms. She sat up and the fabric slid down her arms and she threw it to the floor. She took off the bra and it landed on the blouse.

She reached up and started unbuttoning his shirt. She could hardly wait to see the rippling muscles that she knew were hidden underneath. When she unfastened the first button and got a glimpse of what was hiding there she was like a kid at Christmas. She couldn't wait to unwrap the rest of the package.

She tore through the rest of the buttons and slipped the shirt off his shoulders. The taut suntanned skin that was revealed did not disappoint her. She ran her fingers across his chest and felt him tense, but in a great way.

Trevor leaned forward, pressing her back against the bed once more. Her hand slipped from his chest and she wrapped her arms around his neck, pulling him down with her.

She felt the bulge in his jeans against her leg. It was big and very hard. *My God*, she thought, *that feels enormous*.

Trevor kissed her neck just under her chin. He kept kissing her at one-inch intervals, traveling south, until her reached her left nipple which he took into his mouth and sucked greedily.

Molly arched her back and moaned. Trevor moved his right hand to the waistline of her jeans and started fumbling around trying to find the button. He found it and with one motion, almost like snapping his fingers, he unfastened it.

THE HIGH COUNTRY

He pulled down the zipper as his lips left her nipple. He grabbed the waistline of her jeans with both hands and removed them and her panties in one fluid motion.

The sight of her naked before him made his cock twitch. It was wanting to be released from the confinement of his jeans.

All in good time, he thought. Right now, he wanted to taste the delicacy that just presented itself to him.

Lifting her hips, he dipped his head and placed his lips over the folds of skin that covered her most private parts. He licked the folds apart and thrust his tongue as deep as he could inside her.

She moaned and thrust her hips up to meet his probing tongue. This gave Trevor a better angle and he took his two fingers and gently inserted them where his tongue had been not two seconds prior.

His tongue moved to her clit, flicking it as he continued to move his fingers in and out of her.

Molly moaned loudly, arched her back even further and started shaking as the spasms of her orgasm overtook her. She came on Trevor's mouth as he continued thrusting his fingers deeply into her as he sucked her clit.

When he finally came up for air his chin was glistening with her sweet nectar. He stood, still looking at her, and started to unbuckle his belt.

Molly reached out and placed her hand on his. She shook her head and brushed his hands aside. She grabbed the strip of leather and pulled it through the buckle.

She unbuttoned his jeans and slid the zipper down. Taking the top of his jeans in both hands, she pulled them down to his ankles. She grabbed the lower seam of his boxer briefs and yanked them down too. His cock sprang forward and bobbed in front of her face.

She licked the tip, tasting a bit of his pre-cum. Wanting more, she opened her mouth and slid him inside. She pushed forward taking almost the entire length of his shaft down her throat. Molly sucked on the shaft as she leaned back letting him slide across and through her lips.

Trevor moaned as he thrust his hips forward in rhythm to her movements.

"I want you, now," he said. He took her by the shoulders and leaned her back onto the bed. He knelt between her knees and took his shaft in his hand. With the tip of his shaft he caressed the outer folds of skin that covered her soft center.

Molly moaned and moved her hips to match the caresses. All the nerve endings in her body were tingling with every touch his cock made with her clit.

Trevor took his cock and slipped it between her sweet folds and buried it to the hilt inside her. Molly moaned and arched her hips and met the thrust.

She squealed with pleasure as she wrapped her legs around him. She squeezed her heels against his back, pulling him further into her.

Trevor moved his hips slowly and gently at first, but gradually increased the rhythm and frequency of his thrusts as their passion peaked.

Trevor arched his back and moaned as his seed erupted into her. Molly quivered as the spasms of her own orgasm overtook her once more and she squirted around his shaft. Trevor grunted as the last of his seed spilled into her.

He was looking down at her and saw Molly twitching with intense pleasure and he felt the warm gush as she came. He bent and kissed her tenderly. Molly opened her mouth and granted his tongue permission to enter. Their tongues entwined again as Trevor lay down on the bed beside her. Molly raised her head and Trevor slipped his arm underneath her neck. Molly sighed and rested her head on his chest. Within minutes, Trevor heard Molly's breath even out. She had fallen asleep.

He kissed her forehead tenderly and closed his eyes. Almost immediately Trevor also fell asleep. He was still holding Molly tightly.

CHAPTER EIGHTEEN

TREVOR WOKE THE next morning to the smells of bacon and coffee. He threw back the covers of the bed and sat up. Looking around the room for his clothes he found them strewn across the floor.

His pants were under the window while his shirt was on the floor next to an arm chair. He had trouble finding his boxers. They had been kicked under the bed.

Once he had found all his clothes he got dressed and followed the smells to the kitchen. He found Molly standing at the stove sipping a cup of coffee and turning the bacon in a frying pan. Hearing him come in she turned to face him.

"Good morning," she said. "Trust you slept well."

"I did actually," he replied. "A bit too well I'm afraid."

"I tried not to wake you," she admitted. "I was hoping to feed you breakfast in bed."

"Sorry to disappoint you. Right now, though, I'd just love a cup of that coffee," Trevor said.

"Sir, nothing about you could ever disappoint me," she said, blushing. She turned back to the stove and reduced the heat under the frying pan.

"How do you like your eggs?" she asked.

"Scrambled with a touch of cheddar cheese," he replied. "Then sprinkled with hot sauce."

"But first, I need to call Emily," he said. "I was expected back last night." At the words 'last night' Molly blushed again.

"It won't take but a minute," he continued as he walked to the patio door and stepped outside.

Molly went to the fridge, got the eggs and sat them on the counter.

She looked at the door that Trevor had just walked through. She couldn't stop smiling.

I'm in love with that man, she thought.

Emily was walking into the kitchen as the phone on the wall started ringing. She answered it on the third ring.

"Brigston residence," she said into the receiver.

"Emily, it's me," Trevor said. "I was just calling to check on everyone. How are things going there?"

"Everything is fine here, sir," she replied. "Caroline is already out at the stable. Couldn't interest her in her breakfast until she was assured that her horse had something first."

"That's my girl," he replied. "Just like Ellie Mae looking after her critters."

"I was getting ready to call her in to eat," said Emily. "Eli is still sleeping. He had a rough night last night. He had several coughing spells. I gave him some of his cough syrup and it stopped. He's sleeping it off."

"I'll be home in about an hour," Trevor said. "Do you think he needs to go to the doctor?"

"No, sir," she replied. "I think it's just from the pollen. It's bad this year."

"Okay, but let me know if he flares up again and I'll take him to an urgent care."

"I don't really think that will be necessary, but I'll keep a close eye on him," Emily said.

"Alright, see you in about an hour then," Trevor said.

"Yes, sir. Good-bye," Emily said and placed the receiver back into its cradle.

Caroline burst into the kitchen as Emily took her hand off the phone. She ran to the table, taking her seat.

"Oh no you don't missy," Scolded Emily.

"What did I do?" asked Caroline, puzzled.

"You know the rules of this kitchen as well as I do," Emily said.

"Oh yeah," said Caroline as she stood and went over to the sink. "I forgot to wash my hands after I fed Chocolate."

"That's my girl," said Emily as she put Caroline's breakfast on a plate and put it at her spot on the table. After washing her hands Caroline sat back down at the table.

It may not be any of my concern, Emily thought, *but I'm pleased that Trevor never came home last night. Good for him.*

After finishing his phone call, Trevor stepped back inside the house. Molly had already plated their meal and had it set festively on the table.

"You didn't need to go to all this fuss," Trevor admonished.

"It was no trouble at all," Molly answered. "I told you I love to cook. Especially for you." She blushed slightly, but quickly recovered.

"Everything alright at home?" she asked.

"Caroline can hardly pry herself away from her horse," replied Trevor. "Eli had a rough night. He and Emily didn't get much sleep. He kept having coughing spells."

"Poor baby," she said. "Hope he's okay."

"Emily said he shouldn't need a doctor, but only time will tell," he told her. He quickly changed the subject.

"Looks delicious," he said, looking at the plate before him.

"Hope so," she said. "It's just as you specified, sir."

"Thank you for everything, he said with a twinkle in his eye.

Molly blushed again, but didn't say anything as she sat down at the table as well.

After the meal Molly stood and took the plates to the sink.

"I'll wash them later," she said as she wiped her hands on a dish towel.

"I hate to eat and run," Trevor said. "I told Emily I'd be home within the hour."

"I don't mind," she said. "I know that you have other responsibilities and I understand that."

"I'll call you soon," he promised.

"You'd better," she said.

Trevor pulled her close, kissed her tenderly and turned and walked out the door. Molly turned back to the sink and started running the water for the dishes.

I need to start a load of laundry, she thought, *I don't have anything to wear to work tomorrow.*

Trevor pulled into the driveway as Caroline came running out of the stable, yet again.

"DADDY!" she squealed as she ran to meet his truck.

"Hey Pumpkin," he said as he shut the door. "What have you been up to?"

"Just giving Chocolate a few more carrots," she replied. "You know how much she likes them."

"Gonna spoil her, you are," he answered.

"Nah, she's just hungry," she responded.

"With how many times you give her carrots?" he asked. "How could she possibly still be hungry?"

Caroline laughed, took his hand and together they walked toward the house.

Emily was watching from the kitchen window as she washed the breakfast dishes. What she was seeing made her smile.

Trevor and Caroline walked into the kitchen as Emily was rinsing the frying pan and putting in the drainer. She dried her hands on a dishtowel and turned to face them. Eli was sitting in his high chair with his breakfast smeared all over his face.

"Would you like something to eat sir?" she asked. "I can whip you up something really quick."

"No, thank you, Emily," he answered. "I've already eaten. I know you have been so busy with the kids and everything. Why don't you take the rest of the day off? You have been working so hard and you deserve some time to yourself without having to worry about us."

"Thank you, sir," Emily replied as she wiped the mess from the baby's face. "But are you sure?"

"Yes, ma'am," he replied.

"Then I think I might go and visit my daughter over in Laramie," she said.

"Tell her we said hello," he said.

"I'll do that," she said. "And thank you again. I'll pick up the shopping on my way home this evening."

She took off her apron, folded it and put it on the counter. Picking up her keys she headed to the door. She turned back to them before she spoke.

"Eli seems to be feeling better, no more coughing," she said. "And you might wanna keep an eye on the weather. Morning report said a storm front is coming through. Possibly another bad one."

"Thanks for the head's up," he said. "I hadn't heard. You need to be careful. The roads could get bad."

"I will, and I guess I'll see you guys later tonight," Emily said as she walked out the back door.

"BYE!" shouted Caroline at the closed door. Emily heard her and smiled again as she made her way to her car. It had been over two months since she had visited Tammy, her oldest daughter.

We have a lot of catching up to do, she thought.

At 8:30 p.m. Trevor fed the children their dinner. After dinner he and Caroline cleared, cleaned and put away the dishes. Eli played with a toy car on his high chair tray.

After they finished with the dishes Trevor took Eli upstairs to give him his bath. He washed his hair and tried to run a soapy washcloth over Eli's squirming body. It was pretty much hit-or-miss. All the child cared about was how big of a splash he could make, soaking Trevor in the process.

Trevor got him out of the tub and wrapped a towel around the wet and squirming little boy.

He was running a towel over the baby's hair when he heard the distant roll of thunder. It was followed a few minutes later by a bright flash as a streak of lightning lit up the sky.

"Caroline!" Trevor shouted down the hallway to his daughter.

Caroline peaked her head around the door jam.

"What Daddy?" she asked.

THE HIGH COUNTRY

"You need to hurry and get your bath. Be quick about it because there is a storm coming. Don't forget to brush your teeth," he said. "If you need anything I'll be in the nursery getting your brother ready for bed."

"Will you read us a story?" she asked.

"You bet," he replied as he took the baby and left the bathroom. "Try not to make too big of a mess in here, will ya?"

"I'll try," she promised. She started the water and stepped inside.

Trevor walked over to the crib and lay Eli down on his back. He went to the chest of drawers to get Eli's pajamas and a diaper. When he turned back to the crib he was surprised to see what looked like a water fountain inside the crib. Eli was urinating all over himself and the crib sheets.

"Really?" Trevor asked the child as he looked at the mess.

"Your sister will be in here any minute expecting her story and now I'm having to change your sheets," Trevor complained to the child. Eli was oblivious to the complaint looking up at Trevor cooing.

"Dada, Dada," Eli said, holding his arms out to his father. Trevor scooped up the baby up and lay him down on his back on the floor. Trevor took baby wipes, cleaned and diapered the child and set about to changing the crib sheets.

He pulled the crib sheets off and tossed them on the floor. Getting a fresh set of crib sheets out of the dresser he put them on the changing table.

He took a can of Lysol, he sprayed down the mattress and wiped it dry with the towel that Eli had been wrapped in.

As he was replacing the sheets, Caroline walked into the nursery. Her hair was a tangled mess and there were soap suds mixed in amongst her locks. She was wrapped in a brown bath towel. He looked down at his daughter.

"Did you finish your bath?" he asked, already knowing the answer.

"Yep," she answered.

Trevor touched his daughter's hair and came back with a handful of suds.

"Let me get your brother's pajamas on and I'll help you rinse that soap out of your hair," he said. "Then we'll try to tame those tangles."

"Emily always helps me with my bath," Caroline said. "She washes my hair first 'cause the bath water gets too soapy."

"Now you tell me," said Trevor. "Why don't you sit down in the rocker for now until I get him squared away." Caroline did as she was told, wrapping the towel tighter around her small frame as she took her seat.

Trevor finished dressing his son and pulled up the side rail of the crib. No sooner than the rail clicked into place, Eli was standing up and clinging to the footboard.

"You behave for just a minute," he told Eli. "I have to take care of your sister."

Trevor looked over to the rocking chair, Caroline was shivering.

"Come on, Pumpkin," he said holding out his hand to the child.

She took the offered hand and together they went back into the bathroom. As Trevor walked over to the bathtub the bathmat squished under his feet. Caroline's clothes were soaked from the amount of water on the floor. Bubbles covered the entire tub floor.

"What's all this?" he asked.

"I wanted a bubble bath," Caroline answered.

"What did you use to make the bubbles?" Trevor asked.

Caroline pointed to a plastic bottle on the side wall of the tub. Trevor took the bottle and shook it. It was empty.

"How much if this did you use?" he asked.

"All of it," she answered dutifully.

"But we just bought this bottle," he said. "No wonder you couldn't get all of the soap out of your hair."

He started running fresh water into the tub, but the suds inside the tub kept getting bigger the more the water ran.

"Tell you what," said Trevor. "Why don't we go to my bathroom and let you take your bath there? Would you like that?"

"Can I have another bubble bath?" she asked.

"I think you have had enough bubbles for one night. Don't you?" he asked.

Caroline just shrugged her shoulders as she followed her father into the master bathroom. Trevor ran the water in the tub, checking the temperature. As soon as the water was deep enough, Caroline stepped inside the tub.

Trevor took his shaving cup to the side of the tub and sat down. Dipping the cup into the water he poured the clean water over the suds in his daughter's hair. A big wave of bubbles hit the water with a loud splash. Dipping the cup again he repeated the action until it didn't come back sudsy.

"Okay," said Trevor. "I think that'll do it." Trevor got a fresh towel from under the vanity and handed it to Caroline.

She took it, rubbing it over her head and body. The action of rubbing the towel across her head compounded the tangles that she already had.

Trevor read her and Eli their bedtime story as he was combing through Caroline's hair trying his best to detangle the knots without hurting her. Caroline's job was holding the book and turning the pages. Halfway through the story Eli lay down and closed his eyes. Within moments he was sound asleep.

Trevor finished reading the story long before all the tangles were gone. It another thirty minutes before the comb slid smoothly through her hair. It was almost dry when they finished. He walked with her to her room and tucked her in tight.

Shutting off the light as he left the room. He still had the mess to clean in the kid's bathroom, but instead he went downstairs and straight to the kitchen to fix himself a scotch on the rocks.

Going to the living room he sat down in his favorite recliner, in the dark.

He was sitting there sipping his scotch slowly when he saw the headlights of Emily's car shining through the window. He looked at his glass. It needed refilling. He entered the kitchen as Emily came through the mudroom with an armload of groceries. She sat them on the counter and looked at Trevor.

"Tammy sends her love," she said as she started putting the groceries in the bags away. "How did it go with you guys today?"

"There's a mess in the kid's bathroom I still have to clean and urine stained crib sheets that need to go in the wash." he said

Trevor poured another scotch and said, "Remind me to give you a raise."

"That bad huh," she said grinning.

Trevor only grunted as he left the room and went back upstairs.

He still had work to do.

CHAPTER NINETEEN

THE STORM RAGED outside and the wind howled fiercely. Trevor was sleeping peacefully, that is until a loud noise startled him awake. It had sounded like some type of explosion.

He ran to the window and looked outside. The loft of the barn was on fire. *It must have been a lightning strike*, he thought. He hurriedly got dressed.

I have got to get to the horses, he thought. He ran down the hall to Emily's room. Not standing on formality he barged into the room. He touched Emily's shoulder and she awoke with a start. Realizing that it was Trevor she relaxed, but only a little.

"What's wrong? Is it Eli?" she asked groggily.

"I need you to call 911. The barn is on fire," Trevor instructed. "Then I need you to make sure the children are safe. I am going to try to set the horses out to pasture and fight the fire as best I can until the firetruck gets here."

"Yes, sir," said Emily as she picked up the receiver of the phone on her bedside table and started pushing buttons before he had even left the room.

Trevor ran down the stairs, two at a time. By the time he made it to the stalls the smoke in the barn was thick. The horses were kicking and neighing in a panic. Trevor knew that the loft of the barn was full of dry hay and that it was probably already on fire as well.

He was running out of time. He ran to the tack closet, found a towel and dipped it into chocolate's water bucket. Knowing the horse was terrified, he threw the towel over her face and led her out the side door to the open pasture. He pulled the towel off and slapped her smartly on her hind quarters. The horse jumped and started running for the open pasture. He went back for Maverick.

Maverick was tossing his head and snorting as the smoke stung his nostrils. Trevor dipped the towel into the water again and draped it over Maverick's face and led him to the side door. He yanked the towel off and slapped the horse's rump. Maverick ran to join Chocolate in the pasture.

Trevor turned on the water to the hose lying near the tack room. He started spraying the rafters of the barn, hoping to somehow combat the flames. He started spraying everything in sight, wetting it down in an attempt to save it from the blaze.

He knew that it was probably too late, but he had to try. The fire broke through the floor of the loft as Trevor continued his efforts, spraying where he saw the flames.

In the distance he heard the sirens, the firetruck was on its way. He heard a loud crackling and popping sound. The floor of the loft had given way.

Trevor threw up his arm as the wood splintered and covered him with charred and burning debris. A piece of the timber hit him on the head. Everything went dark and he went down in a heap.

Emily stood with the children on the front porch awaiting the firetruck. The rain had slowed to a drizzle. Eli was still sleepy and rested his head on her shoulder. Caroline paced nervously.

THE HIGH COUNTRY

"Where's Daddy?" she asked looking up at Emily.

"He's trying to save the horses," Emily answered. Looking out across the corral, she saw Chocolate emerge from the barn, run through it and out to the open pasture.

"See," said Emily. "There goes Chocolate."

"Where's Maverick?" Caroline asked. No sooner than those words were spoken Maverick emerged from the barn and ran toward the pasture.

"There he is," Caroline shouted happily. "Now it's Daddy's turn." Caroline waited anxiously for Trevor to appear.

Emily looked up as she heard a loud pop followed by crackling sounds as a corner of the barn collapsed in flames, with Trevor still inside.

"DADDY!" screamed Caroline as she started to run toward the barn. Emily held her back.

Caroline looked up at Emily, anger flashing in her eyes.

"Daddy is in there!" she said. "We have to help him."

The wail of the sirens was getting closer as Emily looked down at the small child.

"Help is on the way," Emily said. "We have to wait on the firefighters. They're coming to help your father."

Comforting the child did little to assuage her own fears. Emily uttered a prayer as she watched the scene unfold before her.

Lord, please let him be alright, she prayed.

The wail of approaching sirens woke Cliff Gordon from a sound sleep. He reached for his glasses on his bedside table. Putting them on as he rose to go look out the window. The movement of him getting out of the bed woke his wife, Ruth.

"What are you doing up Cliff? It's two in the morning," she complained.

"Didn't you hear them?" he answered her question with one of his own as he turned to face her.

"Hear what?" she asked.

"The sirens," he said. "Sounded like they were getting closer."

Before Ruth could answer the room was enveloped in red and white strobing lights and the noise of the sirens was deafening. As quickly as they appeared, the noise started to diminish.

Cliff ran to the window to try to get a view of where they might be going. It looked to him like they might be headed to The High Country.

Cliff ran to the closet and pulled out a pair of jeans and a button up short sleeve shirt. He dressed quickly and turned to face his wife.

"I'm gonna drive out toward The High Country. I think they're headed that way," he said. "If it's not then I'll turn around. If it is, maybe I can help. I know Trevor would do the same for me."

Ruth got up and went over to her wingback chair and picked up her robe that was draped across one of the arms. She wrapped it tightly around her and cinched the belt tightly with a square knot.

"I guess I'll start a pot of coffee," she said. "If it is The High Country I won't be able to get back to sleep until you're home safe. If it isn't, *you* won't be able to get back to sleep."

"I'll call you and let you know what I find," he promised.

"You'd better," she scolded. "Otherwise I'll be a nervous wreck until you get back."

Emily was still standing outside on the porch with the children when the fire engine and hook and ladder truck

THE HIGH COUNTRY

pulled into the driveway. It slid to a halt with a loud hiss of the air brakes.

Three firefighters in full turn out gear jumped from the back of each truck. All of them started pulling the large hoses from the back of both trucks.

Emily ran up to the closest man, Eli and Caroline in tow.

"Mr. Brigston is still in there," she said, pointing to the barn. "He went in to save the horses, but never came back out."

"Larry, you, Charlie and Jim stay on the hoses. Brad, you and Sam get your respirators. Looks like we've got a someone inside," he instructed. Larry nodded and ran off to inform the others.

"Don't worry ma'am we'll find him," he assured Emily as he too started pulling hoses from the truck.

Charlie and Jim ran to the nozzle of the hose and Charlie flipped the lever to start the flow of water. The pressure of the water through the hose was enough that it took two men to hold it steady. The water erupted from the hose and Charlie directed the flow into the heart of the blaze.

Brad and Sam went to the door of the barn and switched on their flashlights. Smoke was billowing out of the entrance as they made their way inside. They began calling to Trevor.

"MR. BRIGSTON!" Brad shouted as they made their way through the dense smoke. Sam went left while Brad went to the right. Panning their lights as they made their way through the darkness. Suddenly Brad's light hit on something. It was a man lying on his side. He wasn't moving.

"OVER HERE!" Brad shouted to his partner. Sam ran to where Brad stood at Trevor's side. Brad directed the light toward Trevor's feet and noticed that his right leg below the knee lay at an odd angle.

"Looks like we have a bad break here," he said. Brad keyed up his portable radio.

"We found him. We need a portable stretcher in here. He's got a bad break and is unconscious," he said.

"Roger that," Captain Ferguson replied. "Greg get that stretcher off the engine. You're going in to assist."

"Got it," Greg Landers replied as he ran to do as he was instructed. He pulled the stretcher off the rack on the back of the truck, donned his respirator and ran into the burning building. The flames were starting to shift and there was still a lot of smoke coming from the barn.

"WHERE ARE YOU!" he shouted as he entered the structure.

"OVER HERE!" was the shouted response.

Greg ran toward the sound of the voice. He found the other men and crouched beside the injured man.

"Okay," said Brad. "Greg, slide the stretcher under him and then on my count, we'll roll him onto his back. Sam, you take his feet. Try to lay the injured leg on the good one. Keep it from moving too much. One, two, three."

Once the stretcher was in place, and on Brad's count, they slowly rolled him down. Greg took one side at the head of the stretcher, Brad the other. Sam took both handles at the foot having assured himself that the broken leg was secured.

"Again, on my count," said Brad, "One, two, three."

All three men lifted and slowly made their way out of the burning structure. As soon as they were clear of the building and in no imminent danger they placed the stretcher on the ground.

Captain Ferguson had requested an ambulance as soon as he had learned of the entrapment. It was pulling into the driveway as the stretcher hit the ground.

Two paramedics jumped out of the vehicle with trauma kits and ran to Trevor.

"What have we got?" one of them asked. Brad was the first to speak.

"He was unconscious when we found him. His right leg is badly broken and he's suffering from smoke inhalation. He also has a laceration on his head. We've only just now got him out. Didn't have time to check him further," he replied.

THE HIGH COUNTRY

"Let's get him on oxygen and a large bore IV saline," The paramedic said as he opened his trauma kit and started removing the required equipment.

"We'll need to get that leg stabilized. We also need to get him hooked up to a cardiac monitor," he continued. An oxygen mask was placed over Trevor's face and the strap was fitted around the back of his head.

"We can do the rest in the bus," the other paramedic said. "We need to get moving with him, NOW!"

The paramedics lifted the portable stretcher and carried it to the back of the ambulance. One of the firefighters opened the rear door and the man at Trevor's head climbed in as he guided the portable stretcher onto the gurney. The other paramedic only got in far enough to assist with getting the stretcher in. Once that was done he got out and closed the door. He ran to the driver's door and got in.

With the sirens blaring, the ambulance roared away into the darkness.

Emily could only watch and pray as the rest of the barn collapsed in on itself, still on fire. She turned and took the children back inside the house.

CHAPTER TWENTY

AS SOON AS the ambulance was in motion Chad Mason, the paramedic in the back with Trevor, tried to start the large bore IV in Trevor's arm. The needle had barely touched Trevor's arm when there was a sudden jolt sending Chad bouncing around in the back.

"Hey! Watch it will ya!" he said. "I almost started this line in his chest thanks to that bump."

"Tell that to the county road crew. Maybe then they can find the funds to finally get rid of all these potholes," answered the driver, David Booker.

"Could you at least manage to dodge a few of them?" Chad said sarcastically.

"Will do," David answered. "Did you get that line in?"

"Going in now," Chad answered. After starting the IV line he reached into one of the upper level cabinets and removed a set of electrodes for the portable EKG monitor on board. He attached them to Trevor's chest and plugged them into the machine. A rhythmic beeping issued from the device. He lifted each of Trevor's eyelids. He shined his small flashlight into Trevor's eyes.

THE HIGH COUNTRY

"I'm calling it in to the hospital," said David. "What have you got?" Chad looked at the monitor.

"Blood pressure is a little low. It's 105/50 and his pulse is 55," he answered. Taking the stethoscope from around his neck, he put the earbuds in place. He listened to Trevor's chest. He didn't like what he heard.

"He has bi-lateral rhonchi. Breath sounds are very raspy. He inhaled a lot of that smoke. Pupils are equal and reactive," replied Chad.

David picked up the microphone of the radio attached to the console of the vehicle.

"Med. 14 to Cheyenne Memorial," he said.

"Cheyenne Memorial base, go ahead," was the reply.

"We are inbound with a male patient approximately 38 years old, 6'2", around 200 pounds. Severe fracture of the right lower leg. Contusions to the face and head. He is also suffering from smoke inhalation. Patient is unconscious at this time. BP is 105/50, pulse is 55. Patient is also presenting with bi-lateral rhonchi. Pupils equal and reactive. We've started an IV with normal saline and have him on oxygen," said David.

"Clear," said the base operator. "We'll be ready for you when you get here. Base out."

As Cliff got close to High Country he pulled off the side of the road to allow an ambulance to pass. It was speeding down the highway in the opposite direction, lights flashing, sirens wailing. That was never a good sign.

He was now convinced that something had happened at the Brigston's. He increased his speed. When he topped the next hill, he saw a glow against the night sky. It was in the area of High Country. All Cliff could think of was the Brigston children.

As Cliff approached the driveway he was able to relax, but just a bit. It wasn't the ranch house that was ablaze, but the barn. The fire trucks were still spraying the barn but it was fully engulfed and a total loss.

Cliff pulled his truck around behind the ladder truck and killed the engine.

He jumped out and ran to the nearest firefighter. She turned when he tapped her on the shoulder.

"What happened here? Who was in the back of that ambulance?" he asked.

"Are you family?" she asked.

"No," Cliff admitted. "I own the neighboring ranch."

"Well, I'm sorry sir, but I can't discuss it," she said. "Maybe you should talk to the lady inside." His concern grew again when he realized the 'lady' she was referring to was Emily. That left Trevor or one of the children. He paled at the thought of something happening to one of the children.

He ran up the steps of the porch and pounded on the door. Emily was still up awaiting news of Trevor's condition. Thinking it was one of the firefighters she opened the door, surprised to see Cliff instead.

"Mr. Gordon," Emily said. "What are you doing here?"

"I woke up when I heard the sirens and thought the firetrucks might be headed this way. What happened? Please tell me it's not one of the children." He blurted.

"The children are fine," she told him. "It's Mr. Brigston. He was in the barn when it collapsed."

"How bad is he hurt?" Cliff asked.

"I don't know," she admitted. "I thought you were one of the firefighters coming to tell me news from the hospital."

"Is there anything my wife or I could do to help?" he asked.

"Pray for him please," she said. "Both of you."

"I'll call our pastor as soon as I get home," he promised. "We'll get a prayer chain started. I have always believed in the power of prayer."

THE HIGH COUNTRY

"Bless you, sir," she said. "I don't mean to be rude, but I just got the children back to bed. I'd hate to wake them again."

She started to close the door, but Cliff put his hand on the door. Emily stopped and looked at him.

"If there is anything that you need we're only one phone call away," he said. "Anytime, night or day."

"Thank you," she said as she closed the door.

Walking back to his truck he took his phone out of his pocket.

He had promised to call Ruth.

The ambulance pulled to a stop in front of the emergency entrance to Cheyenne Memorial hospital and David shut off the lights and siren and jumped out.

He ran to the double doors on the back of the ambulance and swung them open wide. Grabbing the end of the gurney he pulled it toward the open door.

Chad rose and followed the gurney out the door, staying at Trevor's head. Once it had cleared the floor of the ambulance the legs extended and they were able to roll it through the double doors of the emergency room.

David looked at one of the nurses behind the desk.

"Where do you want him?" he asked.

"Med. 14 right?" she asked. David nodded.

"Trauma 2," she said as she rose and led the way to the trauma bays.

"Right in here," she said. "I'll go get the doctor."

A few minutes later there was a flurry of activity as the doctor and trauma team surrounded the gurney.

"We'll shift him on three," said David. "One, two, three."

Now that the patient was on the trauma bed, David and Chad took this as their cue to leave the patient in their capable hands.

"Until next time guys," David said as he and his partner wheeled the now empty gurney back to their waiting ambulance.

David reclaimed the driver's seat, while Chad was relegated to shotgun.

"All in a day's work," said Chad as he picked up the microphone for the unit.

"Med. 14 Radio," he said.

"Go ahead Med 14," was the response.

"10-8 code 9 to Cheyenne Memorial," was his response.

"Radio's clear," came the reply.

Now that their patient was transferred to the care of the hospital staff, they were clear to return to their normal duties.

Dr. Clark O'Connell stepped up to the bedside and lifted one of Trevor's eyelids and shone his penlight into the eye. The pupil contracted immediately.

"Looks like we don't have an obvious sign of brain damage, but I still want a CT scan as well as an X-rays of that leg, head and cervical spine," he said.

Looking up to the display showing Trevor's vital signs the doctor issued further instructions.

"Let's get him intubated. I don't like the look of that oxygen saturation," he said.

"Right away, doctor," said Marsha, the head nurse.

She went to the phone on the wall and called Radiology as the other nurse in the room assisted with the intubation.

Once the tube was in place, Trevor's oxygen level improved, which was a positive sign.

"Once he gets back from Radiology I want to be notified immediately," he instructed.

"Yes, sir," said the nurse. Dr. O'Connell turned and left the room.

CHAPTER TWENTY-ONE

MOLLY HAD AWAKENED around 4:00 a.m. due to the storm and could not get back to sleep. Instead of continuing to toss and turn, she decided to get out of bed.

She went to the kitchen and started a pot of coffee. She was going to be needing quite a bit of it with what little sleep she had gotten.

Once it had finished brewing, she fixed herself a cup and turned on the local news. She hadn't been able to watch it recently and wanted to get caught up on the local events.

She sat down in her recliner as the screen flashed a video of a building completely engulfed in flames with the words 'recorded earlier' in the top left corner of the screen. Picking up the remote she increased the volume. A reporter was now standing in front a pile of charred rubble.

"We are on the scene at High Country Acres on Longmire Road on the outskirts of Cheyenne where sources say lightning may have struck the building you see behind me earlier this morning. The owner of this building, Trevor Brigston, was taken to a local area hospital with serious but unspecified injuries as well as smoke inhalation.

THE HIGH COUNTRY

Firefighter's worked through the early morning hours but were unable to save the structure. No one else was injured in the blaze. Tune in to our 6:00 a.m. report for further details. Back to you in the studio Roger," the reporter said.

Molly dropped her coffee cup and it shattered on her hardwood floor. Its contents spilling on and around her recliner, but she didn't care. She had to get to the hospital, but first she had to find the right one.

She picked up her phone and placed one of several calls that she needed to make. The first call was to the principal of the school where she taught. There was absolutely no way she was going in today. She needed a substitute. She left a message on the school answering service knowing that it would be heard first thing.

The subsequent calls were to three different hospitals in the Cheyenne area asking about Trevor. She finally found him at Cheyenne Memorial and was told that he was still in the emergency department.

That was all she needed to hear. She grabbed her purse and keys and she was out the door.

She had to get to Trevor.

Dr. O'Connell walked into his office with Trevor's X-rays in his hand. He walked over to a small box on the wall and put one of the films in the holder at the top. He flipped a switch and a light came on illuminating the film.

He looked at the display and frowned. The X-ray was of Trevor's lower leg. He saw that there were two fractures in the fibula and one in the tibia.

The fibula fractures would require corrective surgery. The tibia would heal on its own with the removable cast that would be applied after the surgery.

He pulled that slip of film off the machine and replaced it with another. This film was one of the films from the head and cervical spine series. He studied these films as well.

These ones looked more promising. No skull fracture, only a concussion. However, this was concerning as the patient had not yet regained consciousness.

Emily decided to let Caroline sleep in due to the events of the previous night. She knew that the child would not be able to concentrate on her studies from worrying about her father.

Emily needed to go to the hospital to get more information on Trevor's current condition. There was only one problem. She didn't want to take the children to that environment and she didn't have a sitter. The she remembered what Mr. Gordon had said last night. She decided to take him up on his offer and called him.

Ruth Gordon answered on the third ring.

"Hello," she said.

"Hello, Mrs. Gordon, It's Emily over at The High Country. I hope I am not disturbing you," Emily said politely.

"Not at all Emily. What can I do for you?" asked Ruth.

"Well, Mr. Gordon asked if there was anything you two could do for me and I couldn't think of anything other than prayer at the time. But I have thought of something that I want to ask your help with," Emily said.

"Of course, dear, just name it," Ruth replied.

"It looks like I will need to go to the hospital to find out anything about Mr. Brigston's condition as they refuse to tell me anything over the phone. My question is, would you mind watching the children for me while I go?" Emily asked.

"I'd be glad to," Ruth answered happily. "I can be there in twenty minutes. Will that work?"

"Yes, thank you," said Emily. "I'll try to be back as soon as I can. I know these two can be a handful."

"Take your time," Ruth said. "Don't worry about us. We'll be just fine."

"Thank you," said Emily again as she hung up the phone with, "See you in twenty minutes then, bye."

It was a miracle that Molly didn't get stopped as she sped through town trying to get to the hospital. *Please let him be okay*, she thought. *Maybe the news report was wrong, it happens.*

She was relieved when the hospital finally came into view. Going to the Emergency entrance, pulled into the lot and parked the car. She almost ran through the sliding glass doors. They were slow to open and she impatiently shifted her weight from one foot to the other.

When the doors finally slid out of her way she ran up to the first person she saw, an L.P.N.

"Trevor Brigston, is he here?" she asked.

"Are you a relative?" the nurse asked.

"I'm his girlfriend," Molly lied. The nurse consulted her computer screen briefly before looking back up at Molly.

"He's in Trauma 2," the nurse replied. "Down the hall second door on the right."

"Thank you," said Molly as she started in that direction.

Molly opened the door to the room marked 'Trauma 2' and was shocked by what she saw. Trevor was lying there with all sorts of tubes and wires attached to his body. He had a machine breathing for him. The person lying there did not look like the strong, gorgeous man that she had fallen in love with.

She walked over to the bedside and looked down at his still form. His head was bandaged and his eyes were closed. Tears welled up in her own eyes as she touched his hand.

"Trevor," she whispered softly. His eyes fluttered open and he tried to speak, but the ventilator tube prevented it.

"Don't try to talk," Molly said. "I am going to find a doctor or nurse that can tell me what's going on. I'll be right back, I promise."

Trevor nodded and she ran out of the room to get the answers to her questions.

She went to the nurse's desk and spoke to a man sitting at a computer console.

"I have a few questions about the man in Trauma 2, Trevor Brigston," she said.

"Are you a relative?" the man asked.

"Girlfriend," she lied again, nodding.

"His right leg is broken in three places and will require corrective surgery. He inhaled a lot of smoke and has a concussion. The doctor is concerned because he hasn't regained consciousness yet," he told her.

"He was awake a few minutes ago," she said. The man jumped up from his chair and entered Trauma 2. Sure enough, Trevor was awake. He ran to get the doctor.

"Be back in a minute," he said over his shoulder as he left the room.

When the doctor walked into the room he was followed closely by Emily. She looked at Molly with a puzzled expression on her face.

Dr. O'Connell went straight to Trevor's bedside. Trevor started motioning at the ventilator tube, signaling that he wanted it removed. The doctor shook his head.

"We have to leave that in a little while longer," he explained. "I didn't like your oxygen readings when you came in."

The doctor didn't see Emily enter the room and was somewhat startled when she spoke.

"How long does it need to stay?" she asked. The doctor turned around to face Emily.

"We need him to stay on it at least overnight. We'll have to keep a closer eye on him tonight due to the concussion," he answered. He turned to look at Trevor.

"I'm going to ask you a few of yes or no questions," he said. "I want you to blink once for yes and twice for no. Understand?"

Trevor blinked once.

"Good," Dr. O'Connell replied. "I need to check to see if might be suffering from amnesia. Do you recognize these women and know their names?"

Trevor blinked once.

"Do you remember *your* name?" he asked.

Trevor blinked once.

Encouraged the doctor continued. "Good," he said again. "Now, are you experiencing any pain in your head or neck?"

Trevor blinked twice.

"Excellent," the doctor said. "I know that your leg hurts. It's broken and will require surgery to fix it. We were waiting to schedule it until you regained consciousness. You have a few lacerations that we bandaged and a concussion. We'll have keep a close watch on you tonight because of that. Can't risk you slipping into a coma. Understand?"

Trevor blinked once.

"We'll probably remove the tube in the morning, but I want to make sure that you're getting enough oxygen tonight. You inhaled a lot of smoke."

Trevor blinked once. The doctor looked at the two women and asked both to step outside. He followed them out into the corridor and closed the door.

"The small bone in his lower leg is broken in two places. The large bone is also broken. We have an orthopedist coming in the morning for a surgical consult," he said.

"How long will he have to stay in the hospital after the surgery?" Molly asked.

"At least three days but probably no longer than five," he answered.

"So, after his surgery he'll be on crutches for a while?" Emily asked.

"Yes, probably a minimum of six weeks," he answered. "I asked you two to step outside because I didn't want to put him under any more stress right now. He's already been through enough for one day. He needs to remain calm while he's intubated. Can't risk him pulling that tube out."

"Can I bring his daughter to see him?" Emily asked. "She's worrying herself silly."

"How old is she?" Dr. O'Connell asked.

"She's six," Emily replied.

"Yes, of course," he said. "But please wait until the breathing tube is removed. Seeing him like that might frighten her."

"Do either of you ladies have any more questions for me?" Dr. O'Connell asked. Both women shook their heads.

"Then I'll let you get back to your visit," he said.

He turned and walked back to the nurse's station.

Emily looked at Molly and asked, "How did you know he was here?"

"I saw the story about the fire on the news," replied Molly. "Sorry, but I had to come."

"Don't apologize dear," replied Emily. "He's glad that you're here. I saw it in his eyes." That comment made Molly smile.

"Hold on," said Molly. "Where are the children?"

"Your aunt is with them at the house," Emily said. Molly relaxed.

"Shall we go back in?" asked Molly. "I'm sure Trevor is anxious enough about them as well. We need to put his mind at ease, especially right now."

"Yes, I suppose we should let him know," Emily said.

THE HIGH COUNTRY

Both women turned and went back into the room where Trevor lay with his eyes closed. He opened them when he heard them enter.

Emily walked over to the bedside and touched Trevor's arm. She looked down at him, holding back her tears that were threatening to fall.

"I really hate to leave you sir, but I need to get back to the children," said Emily. "Don't want Ruth to be bald from pulling her hair out before I get back."

That comment got a thumbs-up from Trevor. Emily pointed her finger at him but was smiling at him when she did it.

Trevor winked at her.

"I was told that I could bring Caroline to see you, maybe tomorrow?" she asked. Trevor blinked once in response.

After the overnight observation, Trevor was moved to his private room. Molly never left his side.

The doctor returned during his morning rounds and listened to Trevor's chest. It sounded a lot clearer with fewer rattles and crackles.

"Looks like we can take this extra hardware away," he said. "You don't mind, *do you*?" the doctor asked.

Trevor blinked twice for no.

"Good," replied the doctor. "Just let me get a nurse to help me." He stepped out and returned a few moments later with one of the nurses on duty. Within minutes the tube and connected equipment were removed and Trevor was breathing without any assistance.

"My throat is sore." was the first thing Trevor said.

"That's to be expected," the doctor replied. "We'll let you have some ice chips. That should help. Can you take care of that for me?" he asked the nurse. She nodded and left the room.

"I've spoken with the orthopedic surgeon and the surgery is scheduled for the day after tomorrow. Do you have any questions for me?"

"No, thank you," Trevor said, shaking his head. The doctor turned and left the room to check on his other patients.

CHAPTER TWENTY-TWO

TREVOR'S SURGERY WENT off without a hitch. So well, in fact, that he was released a day earlier than expected. He wasn't allowed to put any weight on that leg until after his post-operative follow-up.

Trevor expected to be on crutches for at least four weeks. What he didn't expect was the obstacle course that the ranch house proved to be.

If he wasn't trying to dodge the furniture it was the children's toys. He thought he was adjusting to the crutches well.

The rest of the household seemed to disagree. Caroline looked up from her coloring when Trevor grunted, accidentally shifted his weight to the right crutch that wasn't planted properly. He fell and landed flat of his butt, on the couch.

He had just stepped on one of Caroline's toys and lost his balance. Had it not been for the couch it would have been disastrous.

"DAMN IT!" Trevor shouted.

"Sorry, Daddy," she gushed. "I thought I got 'em all." She rushed to grab the toy from the floor.

Emily gave him a very stern look. One that he knew all too well.

"No, Pumpkin," said Trevor, lowering his voice. "I'm the one that's sorry. I shouldn't have cursed like that. Come here." He patted the couch beside him. Caroline joined him on the couch and Trevor put his arm around his daughter, hugging her close.

"I'm not mad at you," he told her. "It hurt, that's all. But you do have to be more careful with your toys. Someone besides me could get hurt too. Eli could get them and put them in his mouth. He could choke."

"Yes, sir," Caroline said as he lowered her head. "I'll be more careful."

"Now," he said. "Please show me what you were coloring."

Caroline, delighted, ran to get her book. Instead she stopped as she heard something outside and ran to the window. They all heard the loud noises coming from outside.

Emily, too, ran to the window. Her brought her hand to her mouth and turned to face Trevor.

"What's wrong? Has something else happened?" Trevor asked as he got up unsteadily on his crutches.

"Nothing is wrong sir," replied Emily. "Just wait until you see."

Trevor made his way slowly to the window and didn't understand what he was seeing.

Logan was driving a Bob-Cat off a flat-bed truck. He went straight toward the pile of rubble that used to be the barn and began scooping up the charred remains.

Once the front scoop of the machine was filled, he dumped its contents into the back of a dump truck. This continued until all the rubble was cleared away.

Four other trucks were sitting in his driveway. Two of which were also flat-beds. One was loaded with lumber, the other with roofing materials.

THE HIGH COUNTRY

The last two trucks were pickups loaded full, including the bed, with local ranchers and church parishioners.

"What in the world?" he asked. His head cocked to one side as he saw Molly get out of one of the trucks. She looked around at the ranchers and started pointing. The ranchers seemed to be following her instructions.

"Emily," said Trevor. "Can you go find out what is going on?"

"Yes, sir," she replied as she went to the front door.

Emily knew exactly who she needed to talk to. She ran straight to Molly.

"Mr. Brigston has asked me to inquire as to what is going on here," she said. Molly put her hands on Emily's shoulders.

"My uncle started the prayer chain at his church like he said he would. Not only did they pray for Trevor they each started coming forward one-by-one." Molly explained. "Some donated money, others material. And *ALL* of them volunteered their time and labor."

"I don't understand," said Emily, puzzled.

"We're having a barn raising Emily," Molly said joyfully. She threw her head back and waved her arms toward all the building materials being unloaded from the trucks.

"A proper, old fashioned, barn raising. That's what's going on here."

Emily threw her arms wide and wrapped them around Molly in a warm embrace. Releasing Molly, she clasped her hands over her mouth, tears streaming down her face as she ran back toward the house.

"I have to tell Trevor." Was all she said.

Trevor watched the activity from the living room window. The frame work was already in place and a team was working on forming the roof rafters. There was a small rented crane standing by to hoist them into place.

Emily bustled about the kitchen preparing meals for the hungry construction crew. A set of sawhorses had been set up outside and covered with two panels of plywood to form a long makeshift table. Emily had found two white tablecloths to cover the plywood. four clips were attached to each section of the plywood to keep it in place against the wind.

Folding chairs had been brought from the church fellowship hall and were placed around the table and at each end. Trevor would take the place of honor at the head of the table.

The wives of the construction crew were helping Emily with the meal preparations and the duty of carrying the dishes outside.

When the last dish was placed on the table, Emily nodded to Trevor. He took a metal rod and ran it around the large triangle hanging from a hook at the edge of the porch. A loud pinging sound resulted.

"CHOW TIME!" he shouted above the noise.

The hammering stopped immediately. Each man lay down their tools and waited in turn at the water hose to wash the grime from their hands before they took their place at the table. They stood behind their chairs waiting for Trevor to take his seat.

Once Trevor had taken his seat, the rest of the men followed suit. Soon the noise of clattering silverware against china filled the air as the men greedily consumed their meal.

As soon as the men finished the meal, the sound of hammers resounded once more.

The women cleared the table and took everything back inside.

There was work to be done and not just for those outside.

From start to finish the construction of the barn took two and a half days. The entire construction crew were there at sunup and didn't stop working until sundown.

THE HIGH COUNTRY

Trevor stood on the front porch leaning on his crutches admiring the finished structure. The construction team were packing up their gear and clearing away the construction debris.

Trevor thumped one of his crutches on the floorboards of the porch to get everyone's attention.

"I don't know what to say to you," he said. "Thank you doesn't seem like enough when you take into consideration everything that each of you have done for me and my family."

Cliff Gordon was the first of the group to speak.

"I think I speak for everyone here when I say that we have not done anything that you wouldn't have done for one of us," he said. A murmur of approval went through the crowd gathered.

"But we're not through yet," Cliff continued.

"What do you mean? What are you talking about?" Trevor asked. "What more could you do for me that you haven't already my friend?"

"This," said Cliff as a flatbed truck pulled into the driveway and parked. It was fully loaded with freshly baled hay.

"Each ranch here donated at least ten bales of hay," Cliff explained. "We knew that not only did you lose your barn, you lost your hay crop to feed your livestock through the next few months."

"One less thing to worry about," Molly said as she kissed him on the cheek.

CHAPTER TWENTY-THREE

THE TIME HAD come for Trevor's follow-up appointment at the orthopedic surgeon's office. He still couldn't drive, so Molly volunteered to be his chauffeur.

Emily stayed home, looking after the children.

Molly was absentmindedly leafing through a three-year-old Good Housekeeping magazine when Trevor's name was called.

He stood awkwardly and reached for his crutches. Molly beat him to it as she was already holding them out to him.

They followed the nurse down a small winding corridor to a small exam room, where they waited again. The magazines in this room were even older than those in the lobby. Trevor was given a medical gown, told to remove his jeans and have a seat on the exam table. He took off the removable cast so that he could comply with the instructions. Not bothering to put the cast back on, but instead hopped to the exam table

After what seemed like an eternity, the doctor walked in.

"Hello Mr. Brigston," she said. "How have you been doing?"

"Fine, I suppose," Trevor answered. "But these things need to come with warning labels." He held up one of his crutches for emphasis.

The doctor chuckled as she pulled the rolling stool from under the writing desk. She scooted over to the exam table so that she could look at his leg.

She felt around the incision site. Each time she touched an area, she looked at Trevor. Tenderness and swelling could be a sign of infection. Each time she asked. "Does this hurt?" To which Trevor responded, each time, with a "No."

"It's mending well," she told him. "No signs of infection. I'm gonna let you try putting a *little* weight on it. And by 'little' I mean *very little*. Still use both crutches and I'll need to see you again in three weeks. No driving until your next visit. You can make the appointment at the desk on the way out." She shook hands with both of them, turned and left the room.

"Three more weeks on these things," he complained, holding up his crutches.

"At a minimum," Molly reminded. Trevor menacingly, but playfully, shook his crutch at her.

Molly grinned happily as she helped Trevor to his feet and handed him the other crutch.

No sooner than he took it from her, she experienced a severe bout of dizziness. So severe that she had to grab the writing desk to keep from collapsing on the floor.

"Are you okay?" Trevor asked as he was getting dressed.

"I'm fine," she answered. "I just got a little dizzy, that's all. Probably got up too quickly and besides it's gone now."

"Are you sure?" he asked.

"I'm fine," she insisted.

"Well then, shall we head back to the ranch," he said. "There's work to be done. I may not be able to do it yet, but I can still supervise."

"As long as that's *all* you do, supervise," she admonished.

Trevor gave her a sharp look but didn't reply.

Forty-five minutes later, Molly pulled the pickup truck back into the driveway of the High Country Acres and shut off the ignition.

"Wait there," she said. "I'll come around to help."

Trevor opened the door, not waiting for her to help. He was struggling to get his other crutch out of the vehicle when she reached his side.

"I told you that I'd help you," she scolded.

"I can do it myself," he said as he tugged the crutch from the interior of the passenger side. He stood, putting very little weight on his injured leg.

"I see that," Molly replied. "But I'm right here, should you need me."

But he didn't need her assistance. He made it to the porch and up the stairs just fine on his own.

"Daddy!" exclaimed Caroline as soon as she saw her father. She rushed out to hug him, grabbing his legs and squeezing tightly.

"Careful," reminded Molly. "Don't want him to fall."

"It's okay," Trevor said as he patted his daughter on the back. "Where's Eli?"

"He's in the kitchen with Emily," Caroline replied. "He's eating his lunch."

"Have you already had yours?" asked Trevor.

"Yes, sir," she replied. "Didn't get any on me neither."

"Either," Trevor corrected.

"Either," Caroline repeated. The girl looked over to Molly. "Are you staying for lunch Ms. Swanson?"

"No, sweetheart," answered Molly. "And I've told you that away from school, it's okay to call me Molly."

"Why not, Molly?" Caroline asked.

"I have a lot to do at home," she replied. "I need to get back. Maybe another time."

"Okay."

THE HIGH COUNTRY

The little girl skipped away toward the kitchen, leaving the adults in the living room.

Molly waited until Trevor was safely seated in his recliner. She kissed him and turned to leave.

"Thank you for everything you've done," Trevor said.

"You're welcome," she said. "If you need anything else, just call." Trevor raised an eyebrow at this and his smile twisted into devious grin.

"*Anything?*" he repeated.

Realizing what he was talking about, Molly blushed.

"*That* comes after the cast is removed and the doctor has given approval," Molly reminded him as she walked out of the door.

Emily looked up as she heard Caroline skipping into the room.

"Daddy's back," she said. "Ms. Swanson too."

"Is she staying for lunch?"

"No," replied Caroline. "She said she had too much to do."

"Let me finish feeding your brother," Emily said. "Then I'll make a sandwich that you can take to your father. Would you mind helping me with that."

"Can I help make it?"

"I don't see why not."

The child went to the cupboard and removed a loaf of bread. The pair set about making Trevor's lunch.

Molly got home and went straight to work. She had been so busy helping Trevor that she had been neglecting the household chores.

The floors needed to be swept and mopped. The furniture had an inch of dust. She didn't have much to choose from in her closet as most of her clothes were dirty.

After running her sweeper over the floor in the living room, she got a bottle of Pine-Sol from under the kitchen sink. Pulling a mop bucket from walk-in pantry she filled it with water.

She removed the cap of the cleanser and was immediately overwhelmed by the fragrance coming from the bottle. Her stomach lurched, and she felt bile rise in the back of her throat.

Covering her mouth with her hand she ran to the bathroom. There she emptied the contents of her stomach into the cold, porcelain toilet.

Afterwards she sat back on her heels and wiped her mouth with the back of her hand. Slowly she got to her feet and rinsed her mouth with water from the sink. Getting a washcloth from under the vanity she wet it and wiped it across her face.

What is wrong with me, she thought, *I've never had that kind of reaction to that cleanser before.*

Thinking that she might have a stomach bug, she picked up her phone and called her doctor to make an appointment.

They told her that they could work her in the following morning at 10:00 a.m.

CHAPTER TWENTY-FOUR

MOLLY HAD GOTTEN a substitute for the morning hours and since she didn't have to be at the doctor until 10:00, she had slept in. The alarm on her cell phone started blaring at 9:00 a.m.

Reaching for the phone she pushed the snooze button giving her nine more minutes of sleep.

When the strident sounds of the alarm rang again she shut it off and got out of bed.

As soon as her feet hit the floor, she was hit with a sudden wave of nausea. She barely made it to the bathroom where she threw up again.

She rinsed her mouth and brushed her teeth to get rid of the foul taste.

She started the water for the shower and stepped inside.

After completing her shower, she turned off the water. She took the towel that was draped over the shower door and rubbed it over her body and hair trying to absorb the excess moisture.

Before she opened the door, she wrapped the towel tightly around herself. Tucking the corner of it under her arm, she stepped out of the shower.

She caught sight of her reflection in the vanity mirror and didn't like what she saw. A pale, almost ashen, face looked back at her.

Definitely has to be a stomach bug, she thought.

Molly got dressed, picked up her keys and headed to the doctor's office.

Thirty minutes later she pulled into the parking lot of the Cheyenne Internal Medicine Group. She went inside and approached the desk.

"Can I help you?" said the woman behind the counter. A woman whose hair was tied up in a sloppy bun and it looked as though she had spilled most of her coffee on her blouse this morning.

"Yes," replied Molly. "My name is Molly Swanson and I have an appointment at 10:00 a.m."

"Sign here and take a seat," the woman said. "Has anything changed since your last visit?"

"No," answered Molly.

Fifteen minutes later, and halfway through a magazine article, Molly's name was called.

She dropped the magazine in a chair and followed the nurse down the hall to a small examination room. The nurse entered and sat down at a computer on a writing desk. She motioned for Molly to sit on the examination table.

"What brings you here today?" the nurse asked.

"I feel like I might have picked up a stomach virus," Molly replied.

"Nausea and vomiting or diarrhea? Or both?" the nurse asked.

"The former," answered Molly.

"How long has it been going on?" the nurse asked.

"I have been vomiting since yesterday," Molly replied.

"Anything else?" the nurse asked.

"I've had a couple of dizzy spells," Molly admitted.

The nurse looked up from the computer and asked Molly another question.

THE HIGH COUNTRY

"When was your last menstrual cycle?"

Molly had to think for a minute before she answered.

"I haven't really thought about it, but I guess it was about six weeks ago," she answered.

"Any chance that you might be pregnant?" the nurse asked.

Molly blushed at the thought.

"Well, I have been active," Molly admitted. "But I have been on birth control pills."

The nurse was busy typing and looked up again as Molly said this.

"The birth control pills are only 98% effective," she said. She continued to type the information into the computer.

The nurse got up and left the room telling Molly, "The doctor will be with you shortly."

Molly waited another fifteen minutes before the doctor finally knocked on the door. After knocking, the doctor opened the door and stepped inside.

"Ms. Swanson, I'm Doctor Hanson," he said. "Sorry that you're not feeling well. We'll see what we can do to remedy that."

After talking to Molly for a few minutes, the doctor stood and got a medical gown from the cabinet above the sink.

"I want you to put this on," he instructed. "I'll be back with a nurse to complete the examination." He turned and left the room in order for her to change.

What the hell, she thought, *it's just a stomach virus. Give me some anti-nausea drugs and send me home.*

A lab technician came in with a tray containing vials, tubes and needles.

"Ms. Swanson," he said.

"Yes," replied Molly timidly.

"The doctor has requested some routine blood work," he said. "Including a pregnancy test."

"Pregnancy test?" asked Molly.

"Just a precaution," he told her. "To rule it out due to the medication that may be prescribed."

"Oh," said Molly, relaxing a bit.

The blood was drawn and the lab technician left the room. Almost immediately the doctor re-entered the room with a female nurse.

"I looked at your file," he said. "I didn't see a recent PAP smear, so I'll do one today."

"It has been a while," Molly admitted.

The doctor took the samples that were required and asked Molly to sit up. The nurse pushed in the end of the table that Molly had been resting her feet upon.

The doctor already knew what was causing her nausea and vomiting.

"I need you to make a follow up appointment for one week from now," the doctor said. "We should have all of the test results back by then."

"Okay," said Molly, looking confused. "But what about the nausea in the meantime?"

"Keep some saltine crackers by your bedside and eat a few before you get out of bed in the morning," he answered. "That should help with the morning sickness."

"*Morning sickness?*" she repeated, stunned.

"Yes, ma'am," he replied. "I am pleased to tell you that you're pregnant. About four weeks along I'd say."

"I want you to start one of these prenatal vitamins," he said as he handed her a sheet of paper containing a list of supplements. "But only one."

"Thank you," she said as she took the paper.

"You'll need to make an appointment with an obstetrician as soon as you can. Do you need a referral?" he asked.

"Please," she said. The doctor handed her another piece of paper with a list of OB/GYN doctors.

Molly took the offered paper and put both lists on the table beside her.

THE HIGH COUNTRY

"We'll call you with the test results when they come in," he said. "We'll also send a copy to the obstetrician you choose. I'll need you to sign this permission form for the sharing of information."

"Get dressed and stop at the front desk," he continued. "I'll give this form to the desk clerk."

Molly thanked him as he left the room. After the door closed she dressed quickly and went to the desk as instructed.

The clerk looked up as she approached.

"Can I help you?" she asked.

"I'm Molly Swanson," she answered. "The doctor wanted me to sign a permission form to share information."

"Yes," said the clerk. "I have it right here."

She placed the piece of paper on the counter in front of Molly and handed her a pen.

"I just need you to sign right here," said the clerk, pointing to a line on the form. Molly signed the form and paid her co-payment for the visit.

Her feet felt like they were weighed down with lead on the way back to her car.

How in the hell am I going to tell Trevor? she thought.

Molly stopped at the drug store on her way home and picked up the vitamins that the doctor recommended. She also found a book that she thought might help, 'What to expect when you're expecting'. She also grabbed a box of saltine crackers.

She went to the register and paid for her items. Bag in hand she went back to the car. On her way home, she made a mental list of things that she needed to do.

First on the list, get back to the school. She still had a class to teach.

CHAPTER TWENTY-FIVE

MOLLY MADE THE mistake of trying to step through the doorway of her classroom as the morning recess bell rang. Her students almost ran over her as they ran out of the room toward the playground.

Molly jumped aside, out of the way. When the last student passed her, she managed to actually enter the room. The substitute was standing at the dry erase board running the eraser over it removing the morning's lesson. She turned when she heard Molly come in.

"Oh, hi," she said.

"Thank you for filling in Donna," Molly said. "Wanna fill me in on today's events."

"They've completed the reading assignment and math worksheets," Donna replied as she pointed to the papers on the desk.

"After recess I was planning on the science experiment," Donna continued. "But now that you're back I'll turn them back over to you."

"Thanks, again," said Molly.

"No problem," replied Donna as she picked up her purse and left Molly to her students.

Molly felt another wave of nausea and opened the box of crackers and popped one of them into her mouth. That made it a little better, so she ate another one.

Before she knew it, she had eaten the entire stack.

Trevor hadn't been cleared to drive so he wasn't allowed to operate his farm equipment either. He had no choice but to sit in a chair on the porch, watching Logan and the other ranch hands bringing in his hay crop.

He lifted a bottle of beer to his lips and took a large swig of it. Looking at the bottle he realized something.

If he *was* operating the farm equipment, he wouldn't be enjoying the beer that he held in his hand. Smiling, he thought to himself. *Being injured might have some benefits after all*. He took another large swig.

Emily opened and peeked her head around the screen door. He turned at the sound.

"Sorry to bother you," she apologized. "But I was just wondering if there was anything specific that you might like for dinner sir?"

"You know what?" he asked. "Now that you mention it, I have been craving spaghetti. Maybe some garlic bread too?"

"Sounds good," she said. "I'll get that started right away. Will Ms. Swanson joining us tonight?" Emily asked.

"I was just thinking about calling her," he replied. "Can you make a little extra?" he asked, "Just in case?"

"Yes, sir," said Emily as she turned and went back into the house. Trevor couldn't see the sly smile on her face.

There's just something about that woman, Emily thought, *she will be so good for him and the children*.

She dared not voice that opinion aloud. Instead she kept her thoughts to herself. *Best not to meddle too much*.

Molly didn't go straight home after the school day was over. She was thinking of a clever way to let Trevor know what she had been told this morning.

She stopped at a nearby boutique that sold children's clothing. Inside, she found exactly what she was looking for. Satisfied with her selection, she paid for it and headed back to her car. She was almost to her car when her cell phone rang.

Fishing around in her purse, she finally found it. Not really looking at the screen, she answered it.

"Hello," she said.

"Hello, beautiful," said the husky voice on the other end of the line. Molly pulled the phone away from her ear and looked at the screen. Seeing the name displayed she smiled.

"Hope you're behaving yourself today," she said.

"Now where's the fun in that?" Trevor asked.

"You know what I mean," she scolded.

"Yes," he admitted. "I'm afraid I do. I'm sitting on the porch watching work being done, instead of doing it myself."

"Good boy," Molly said jokingly. "I like men that do as they're told." Trevor grunted softly.

"I heard that," she said. He cleared his throat before he continued.

"I know it's late notice," he said. "But I was wondering if you could come over for dinner tonight? That is, if you don't already have something planned."

"Well," she said. "I haven't even made it home yet, much less had any idea of what to do about my dinner."

"Can I take that as a yes?" he asked.

"Yes," she conceded. "What time?"

"Can you be here in an hour?" he asked.

"I suppose," she said. "That should give me enough time to go home, freshen up and change."

"Good," he said. "See you in an hour."

"Okay," she replied. The phone beeped twice as the call was disconnected.

He called me to ask for a date in the middle of the week, she thought. She suddenly felt butterflies in her stomach.

"Please don't let me be sick again," she pleaded aloud to the empty car.

Molly made it home in record time. She immediately ran to the bathroom and began stripping off her clothing.

She turned on the water to the shower, adjusted the temperature of the water and stepped inside. The coolness of the cascading water helped soothe her stomach as she leaned into the flow

She squeezed a generous amount of body wash into the palm of her hand and put the bottle into the rack hanging from the shower head.

Taking her loofa sponge, she lathered it with the body wash and started rubbing the sponge over her body.

Her hand paused over her abdomen as she thought of the new life growing there.

She'd been planning to tell Trevor over the next weekend, but tonight would be just as good.

Twenty minutes later Molly pulled into the driveway of High Country Acres. She walked up the porch steps and rang the doorbell.

She was pleasantly surprised to see that it was Trevor who had opened the door. He pushed the door open wider and motioned her inside.

"Glad to see you up and about," she said as she stepped across the threshold. "Just hope you're not over doing it."

"You know me," Trevor retorted as he closed the door.

"Yes, I do," she admitted. "Why else do you think I would have said that?"

"If it makes you feel any better," he said. "Emily has been looking out for me in that respect."

"It does," she admitted. "By the way, where is Emily?"

"Her and Caroline are in the kitchen," he answered. "Caroline wanted to make the garlic bread by herself."

Molly put the back of her hand against the side of her mouth.

"*With a little help*," Molly whispered. Trevor winked. She went to the kitchen to find Emily.

"Trevor said I could find you in here," Molly said as she entered the room.

"Yes," Emily replied. "I'm in here most of the time."

"Is there anything I can do to help?" Molly asked.

"No," Emily answered. "We have it all under control. We'll be sitting down to eat in about twenty minutes."

"Well if you both are sure," Molly said.

"We got this," said Caroline.

"Good," replied Molly. "Because I have something to discuss with your father."

"Go right ahead," said Emily. "You have plenty of time."

Molly went back into the living room and found Trevor sitting in his favorite recliner with his leg propped up on a pillow.

"Am I disturbing you?" she asked.

"Never," he said. "Have a seat." He pointed to the chair across the table from himself.

"Good," she said, taking the recommended seat. "I have something that I need to discuss with you,"

"Uh-oh," Trevor said. "This sounds serious. You have my full attention."

Molly had a serious look on her face and it worried Trevor. He had never seen this look before.

"Is everything okay?" he asked, concerned.

THE HIGH COUNTRY

"Well you know that I haven't been feeling well lately," she admitted. "I went to the doctor this morning thinking I had a stomach bug."

"And I'm assuming that the doctor told you that it would have to run its course?" he asked. "Drink plenty of fluids, that kinda stuff."

"Well, it *is* going to have to run its course," admitted Molly. "Just not in the way you're thinking."

"I don't understand," Trevor said. "What are you trying to tell me?"

Molly reached into her shopping bag and removed the item that she purchased before going home this afternoon. She held it up for Trevor to see. It was a t-shirt that looked like it was the right size for Eli.

It wasn't the shirt itself that attracted his gaze. It was what was written on the front of it. It read:

"I'm going to be a big brother."

Trevor brought his hand to his face and rubbed his chin before looking up and into the eyes of Molly. She folded the shirt and put it back into the bag.

"I wasn't planning on actually giving it to him," she said. "Much less expecting him to wear it. I just tried to think of a clever way to tell you."

"But…" Trevor began. Molly put up her hand to stop him.

"Before you say anything," she said. "I'm on birth control. It didn't work."

"But…" Trevor tried once more. Again, Molly interrupted him.

"I know," she said. "You probably didn't plan on having any more children, but I didn't plan on getting pregnant either."

"But…" Trevor repeated.

"Please let me finish," she said. "I can't have an abortion, I won't. I intend to have it."

Molly paused and waited for Trevor to respond. After a few seconds he took the hint.

"*Oh*," he said. "It's okay for *me* to talk now."

"Yes, sorry," she said as she looked down at her feet, expecting the worst.

Instead of saying anything, Trevor got to his feet and with the aid of his crutches shuffled over to where she was sitting.

Molly looked up when she heard him rise. Trevor reached out and took her hand. He kissed her on the cheek and brushed a stray hair away from her face.

"Of course, you're going to have it," Trevor said tenderly. "*We're* going to have it."

Molly looked at him with a puzzled look on her face.

"*We?*" she asked.

"You don't expect me to turn my back on the greatest gift a woman could ever give, do you?" he asked. "The gift of a child."

"But…" Molly began.

"Please, let *me* finish," he said, taunting her with her own words. Molly closed her mouth and didn't finish her sentence.

"I have probably loved you since the moment I first laid eyes on you," he said. "You've done so much for me that I could never begin to thank you enough. And I have something that I want to ask you. Although, you'll have to forgive me for not kneeling."

Molly's free hand went to her mouth and she started shaking. Her eyes glistened from the tears that were forming and threatening to fall.

"Will you marry me?" he asked as he kissed her hand.

Molly jumped from her seat and threw her arms around Trevor's neck almost causing him to lose his balance.

"Yes!" Molly squealed into his ear. Tears flowing freely down her cheeks. They were tears of joy.

THE HIGH COUNTRY

"Okay, then that settles that," he said. "Shall we go to dinner?"

The couple entered the dining room as Emily was placing the last dish on the table. She looked up when she heard them.

"Prefect timing," said Emily. "I was just getting ready to send Caroline in to tell you that dinner is ready. Please take a seat."

Eli was in his high chair and Caroline was already seated. Emily took her seat to the right of the baby.

"Before we do that," Trevor said. "We have an announcement to make."

Emily looked up at the couple, stopping the spoon midway to Eli's mouth. Caroline cocked her head to one side, looking bewildered.

Trevor looked lovingly at Molly.

"I've just asked Molly to marry me," he said.

Emily dropped the spoon and she covered her mouth with both hands.

"And I said yes," Molly said. "So, I guess that means that we have a wedding to plan."

"What do you think sweetheart? Two weeks from Saturday?" she continued.

Emily jumped up from her seat and ran to hug both of them.

"Congratulations," she said as she kissed them both on the cheek. She looked at Trevor before adding.

"And it's about time too."

Molly had an idea that she needed to run by Trevor.

"I need to talk to you about something," Molly said.

"I'm all ears."

"In private, please?"

"Uh-oh, this sounds serious. Let's go to my den." When the got to the den Trevor took a seat in one of the arm chairs. He motioned to the chair opposite him.

"Make yourself comfortable. Now, what's on your mind."

"I was wondering if I could take Caroline shopping with me tomorrow? She'll need a new dress for the wedding and I thought that we could look for one together. Maybe make a day of it." Molly said.

"I think that's a great idea. It would give her a chance to get to know you a little better."

"My thoughts exactly, but don't tell her. I want it to be a surprise."

"What time were you thinking about coming to get her?" he asked.

"Around 10:00 o'clock?"

CHAPTER TWENTY-SIX

MOLLY PULLED INTO the driveway of High Country and shut off the ignition. She sat in the driver's seat for a few minutes thinking.

She was glad that her relationship with Caroline had transformed over the last few weeks. It had been awkward at first coming into Caroline's life as something other than her teacher.

Once Molly had explained that she wasn't trying to be a replacement for Beth, Caroline had seemed to relax a little with her.

She got out of the vehicle and walked up to the porch, taking the steps two at a time.

After ringing the doorbell, she stepped back and waited. She was surprised to see Caroline on the other side of the door.

"Hello, Ms. Swanson."

"Hello, Caroline, and I've told you that you can call me Molly away from school."

"Who is it?" Trevor asked from the living room.

"It's Molly."

At the mention of Molly's name, Trevor was on his feet and headed to the foyer.

"Caroline aren't you going to let her in?" he asked. Caroline stepped back opening the door wider. Molly walked in and turned to face her.

"You're just the person that I needed to see," Molly said.

"*Me?*"

"Yes, you. I'm needing to get me a new dress and I thought you might want to go with me to help me pick it out. Grab some lunch, what do you say?"

Caroline looked up at her father with sad, puppy dog eyes.

"Can I, Daddy? Please?" she pleaded.

"Well, I don't see why not." Trevor conceded. He winked at Molly, who smiled.

"Well then, let's go."

"I've gotta go get my purse," said Caroline as she ran to the stairs. "Don't leave without me."

"I'll be right here," Molly promised.

Thirty minutes later, Molly pulled her car into the lot at the River Walk Mall. She turned off the ignition and they got out of the car.

As they were walking across the parking lot, Molly looked down at Caroline.

"Where should be go first?" she asked.

"Somewhere that sells really nice dresses."

"That sounds like a plan."

They stopped just inside the glass doors and looked at the information sign in the middle of the floor. Molly pointed to a location on the map.

"There's a nice dress store upstairs," she said.

"Well, let's go."

They found the boutique and stepped inside. Caroline ran to the first dress she saw and held it up.

"What about this one?" she asked.

"That one looks like it might fit you. Do you like it?"

"It's pretty."

THE HIGH COUNTRY

"Let's go and try it on," Molly said. They found the dressing room and Molly stood guard as the child put on the dress.

"I'm ready." She stepped out of the dressing room and stood in front of the full-length mirror.

"It is pretty," admitted Molly.

"But it's too scratchy," Caroline complained as she rubbed the back of her neck.

"Okay, go back in and change. We'll look for a different one."

Once Caroline was dressed, she came out of the fitting room. She handed the dress to Molly, who put it on the rack meant to hold the floor returns.

They walked back to the girl's department. This time Caroline felt the material of the dresses before she tried them on. She found one to her liking and they went back to the fitting room.

Once she was dressed, Caroline stepped out to show it to Molly. She stood in front of a full-length mirror again and did a twirl.

"I like this one," Caroline said.

"Good, let's get it. Go back in and change, then we'll go get mine."

Molly had already selected her wedding gown and was actually picking it up at another boutique. Caroline stepped back out of the changing room with the dress over her arm.

"I thought we might go to the jewelry counter," Molly said. "I have a surprise in store for you."

Caroline's face lit up at the mention of a surprise.

"*Really?*"

"Yes, ma'am. Shall we?" Molly reached out and took Caroline's hand. Together they found the jewelry display that Molly was looking for.

On the rack were several lovely, engraved silver lockets.

"This is your surprise. Pick one," Molly said.

Caroline looked at each of the lockets before selecting a heart shaped one. She held it out to Molly.

"Can I get this one?"

"I think it's perfect," Molly replied. "When we get back to the ranch, I'll help you put the pictures in it."

"I want to put a picture of Mommy in it."

"We'll put a picture of your Mommy on one side and one of you on the other. Would you like that?"

"Yeah, I would," Caroline replied, smiling up at Molly.

"That way she'll always be with you."

"I like that. I'll never take it off except at bath time." Caroline wrapped her arms around Molly's waist and squeezed tightly.

"Thank you," she said.

"You're welcome."

They went to the closest register and paid for their selections. They left the store and headed to the food court.

Molly smiled as she looked down at the child holding her hand, both of them looking forward to the future and what was to come.

Right now, though, Molly was thinking about her growling stomach.

"I don't know about you, but I'm hungry," Molly said.

"Can we get pizza?"

"Pizza it is."

CHAPTER TWENTY-SEVEN

MOLLY HAD INSISTED on a small, intimate ceremony with just a few family members and close friends.

She had asked her cousin Marissa to be her maid of honor, while Trevor had given the honor of best man to Logan.

The flower girl honor went to Caroline. Eli was to be the ring bearer.

A large three pole tent was erected in the yard to house the reception. An arch covered with roses would serve as the alter for the ceremony.

A long narrow red carpet ran between two rows of folding chairs that were on loan from the fellowship hall of the local Baptist church. The pastor conducting the ceremony was from the same church and had been contacted by Molly. He had happily agreed to provide his services for the occasion.

Molly was upstairs with Marissa putting the finishing touches on her hair and makeup. Marissa pinned a stray curl back into place with a bobby pin and stood back to admire her work.

"Something still isn't right," she said.

"What's the problem?" Molly asked. "I think it looks fine."

"I've got it," Marissa said, snapping her fingers. "It's the something old, something new deal."

"My wedding dress is the something new," said Molly. "I'm wearing my grandmothers earrings, that's something old. I don't have anything borrowed of blue."

Marissa thought a moment before she reacted. Taking the necklace from around her own neck she fastened it around Molly's.

"My mother gave me this," she said. "The center stone is a blue topaz. That covers the borrowed *and* the blue. Just keep in mind that it *is* borrowed. I'll be wanting it back."

"It's beautiful," said Molly as she admired the reflection in the vanity mirror. "Thank you."

Tears were welling up in Molly's eyes. Marissa noticed and scolded Molly.

"You can't start crying now," she said. "Those tears will ruin the makeup that I spent two hours getting perfect."

Molly took a Kleenex and dabbed in at the corners of her eyes.

"Can't be looking like a racoon on my wedding day," she said.

"Exactly," Marissa agreed. Marissa went to the closet and removed a beautiful, floor length white dress.

The front of the dress was studded with small beaded pearls and sequins. It glistened when the light hit it. It was strapless and the bodice fit her curves perfectly. Below the bodice of the gown, the dress was more loosely fitted.

"Let's get you into this beautiful thing," Marissa said. "Shall we?"

Eli was upstairs with Emily. She had found a tuxedo to fit him online and was giving him a bath to get him ready. His suit was lying on the changing table. Running the towel over the child's head, Emily dropped it into the crib and got the clothing.

THE HIGH COUNTRY

It took her almost ten minutes to get Eli dressed, but when she finished he looked adorable. Tiny patent leather shoes completed his ensemble. He looked he had just stepped out of the baby version of G.Q.

Trevor and Logan were downstairs in his man cave with a few of the male family members. Both of them had already dressed in their tuxedo pants and shirt but not their jackets. They were milling about the room casually engrossed in conversation. A television was on in the corner, but hardly anyone was paying any attention to it.

Trevor paced nervously around the room. Logan stepped up and patted him on the back.

"Are you nervous man?" he asked.

"Wouldn't you be?" Trevor responded to his question with one of his own.

There was a knock on the door and Logan left Trevor went to open it. Standing on the other side of the threshold was the pastor, John Metcalf.

"They're ready for you," he said. Trevor and Logan grabbed their jackets from the back of their chairs and donned them.

"We'll be right there," Logan said. "Are you ready?" he asked, looking at Trevor.

"Ready, willing," Trevor said. "And able."

"Then let's get this show on the road," Logan said. "You guys had better go take your seats," he said to the family members in the room.

The men started filing out, each patting Trevor on the back as they exited the room.

After the family had left, Logan looked Trevor over to make sure that nothing was out of place. Confident that everything was perfect, he looked at Trevor as he opened the door.

"Shall we?" he asked.

"After you," was all that Trevor said.

Molly was adjusting her veil when there was a soft knock on the door. Marissa opened it to find Molly's aunt Ruth standing there. Marissa stepped aside to let her enter the room.

"You look lovely my dear," Ruth said. "I wish your father could be here to see you at this moment. He would be so proud."

"I carry him with me in here," Molly said, patting her chest.

"I just came to tell you that they are almost ready for you," Ruth said. "Cliff is waiting in the vestibule to walk you down the aisle.

"I'll be ready in five minutes," Molly promised.

"Good," replied Ruth. "I guess I'll go get my seat." She kissed Molly on the cheek and hugged her close.

The men had already taken their places on the right side of the rose covered arch while pastor Metcalf stood directly in front of it. They looked expectantly over the gathered guests to the spot where Molly would make her entrance.

Trevor shifted his weight to his good leg. His injured leg had started to ache and he wanted to rest it.

The piped in organ music suddenly changed as he saw Eli toddling up the carpet holding a satin pillow. He started walking faster when he saw Trevor. His father motioned for him to come to him. Eli stopped in front of Trevor and turned and faced the audience.

Marissa came around the side of the barn and walked slowly down the carpet. She took her place on the left side of the arch.

Caroline emerged from the corner of the barn. She made her way to the carpet and started dropping the petals from the basket over her arm. She tossed the last of the petals and took her place on the left side of the arch beside Marissa.

The organ music changed again, this time to the bridal march. Everyone got to their feet and turned to watch Molly and Cliff make their way slowly along the carpet. The train of her dress gently brushing the petals as she made her way to the man of her dreams.

"Who gives this woman to be wed?" the pastor asked.

"On behalf of her father," Cliff said. "I do."

He took Molly's hand and gently placed it into Trevor's. Lifting Molly's veil, he kissed her on the cheek. Taking his seat between Molly's mother and Ruth, Molly saw him wipe away a tear from his eyes. Molly smiled at him.

"Dearly beloved," John said. "We are gathered here today to join this man and this woman in the bonds of holy matrimony. If anyone objects to their union, speak now or forever hold your peace."

The audience was silent.

John turned to Trevor and began the ceremony.

"Do you Trevor," he said. "Take this woman Molly to be your lawfully wedded wife? To have and to hold from this day forward? For better or worse? For richer, for poorer? In sickness and in health? To love and to cherish, so long as you both shall live?"

Trevor turned to Molly when he said, "I do."

John looked at Molly and continued.

"And do you Molly," he said. "Take this man Trevor to be your lawfully wedded husband? To have and to hold from this day forward? For better or worse? For richer or poorer? In sickness and in health? To love and to cherish, so long as you both shall live?"

Molly squeezed Trevor's hand as she replied, "I do."

"Do you have the rings?" John asked. Logan stepped forward and put Molly's ring into Trevor's hand.

"Place the ring on her finger," John instructed. "And repeat after me." Trevor slipped the ring over the tip of Molly's finger and waited.

"With this ring I thee wed," said John. Trevor repeated the words as he slipped the ring the rest of the way onto her finger.

"Now for the other ring," John said.

Marissa stepped forward and put Trevor's ring into Molly's hand. She slipped it over the tip of Trevor's finger and waited.

"Molly repeat after me," John said. "With this ring I thee wed." Molly slid the ring into place on Trevor's finger and repeated the words as instructed.

"By the power invested in me," John said. "I now pronounce you husband and wife. You may kiss your bride."

Trevor wrapped his arms around Molly and pulled her close. He kissed her and the tension he had been feeling drifted away. It was replaced by sheer joy.

"Molly and Trevor," John said. "Will you now face your family and friends?"

The couple turned and faced the audience.

"It is with great pleasure that I present to you for the very first time," John said. "Mr. and Mrs. Trevor Brigston."

Applause erupted from the audience as the couple made their way down the carpet and to the reception tent.

EPILOGUE

MOLLY SAT ON the porch in the early morning hours sipping a cup of coffee. She looked down at the sleeping baby nestled safely in her other arm. Jeremiah Jacob, affectionately known as J.J., was thirteen days old. He was born with a full head of dark brown hair and was the spitting image of his father. Molly hoped that he wouldn't grow out of that.

Caroline sat on the porch next to Molly, looking up at her.

"Can I hold him?" she asked.

"Can you sit in that other chair?" asked Molly. Caroline hopped up and immediately went to the chair. As soon as she was settled she held out her arms.

Molly put down her cup, wrapped her arms around the baby and stood. She gently put the baby in Caroline's extended arms.

"Careful," Molly instructed. "Hold his head."

Caroline started gently rocking the baby, humming under her breath. Molly sat back down in her chair intently watching her step-daughter with her son.

Eli came waddling out the front door and over to where Molly sat. He held his chubby little arms out to her.

"Mommy," he said. They had been working with him to pronounce Molly's name, but it always came out 'Mommy'. She smiled and lifted the child into her lap and held him tight.

"Bubba," he said, pointing to J.J. He had trouble saying brother too.

"Yes," said Molly. "That's your brother."

Trevor stepped out onto the porch and couldn't help but smile as he admired his family, happily sitting there in front of him.

I am a very lucky man, he thought, *very lucky indeed.*

Made in the USA
Columbia, SC
26 January 2019